RAE   **Rae, Harloe, author.**
       Redefining us FRA

7/2018

redefining us

D1520070

HARLOE RAE

ST. MARY PARISH LIBRARY
FRANKLIN, LOUISIANA

Redefining Us
Copyright © 2017 by Harloe Rae
All rights reserved.

No part of this publication may be reproduced, distributed, or transmitted in any form or by any means, including photo-copying, recording, or other electronic or mechanical methods, without the prior written permission of the copyright owner and the publisher listed above, except in the case of brief quotations embodied in critical reviews and certain other noncommercial uses permitted by copyright law.

This is a work of fiction and any resemblance to persons, names, characters, places, brands, media, and incidents are either the product of the author's imagination or purely coincidental.

Cover Design:
Harloe Rae

Editing:
Ace Gray

Proofreading:
Proof This—Proofreading by Jen

Interior Design & Formatting:
Christine Borgford, Type A Formatting

ST. MARY PARISH LIBRARY
FRANKLIN, LOUISIANA

This book is dedicated to
anyone that still believes people can be
saved, no matter how bleak their situation.
I'll always hold out hope right along with you.

I hope you all enjoy Xander & Willow!

prologue
willow

P ain. Debilitating pain is all I feel as I attempt to keep my emotions in check. Saying goodbye to my best friend was never a thought I entertained. Now it's my reality.

"Wills." His voice takes on a pleading tone as he stares into my tear filled eyes. "Please don't make this harder for me than it already is." He continues to look at me as the saltwater drips down my cheeks.

"I'm sorry, X, but you have no idea how difficult life will be here without you." I can't catch my breath as the hysteria threatens to take over. I try to take deep inhales between puffs of pitiful exhales.

He presses his forehead to mine and I don't think he understands how much that involuntary, ingrained move means to me at that moment. Xander is one of the greats and I'm about to lose him.

"Promise me," I begin in a begging voice. "Swear to me that you'll come back and everything will be the same."

"Willow Shae, I could never stay away from you longer than necessary, so you don't even have to ask. But yes, I promise and swear I will be back as soon as possible to return to our regularly scheduled friendship."

With that remark, he has me cracking a smile. Even through the tears. Gosh, I will miss this man.

"Will you write me? Does that sound cheesy? I see it in all the old time movies and I always wanted to say it." Maybe it is the dreamy lilt to my voice that has his lips quirking into a smile.

"Wills, I will write you every chance I get and I expect the same. Now, give me a hug that means everything you feel because I won't see you for at least a year." His eyebrows crease with that devastating blow, even though I'd heard that timeline before. I can tell he's still very worried about how I'm feeling based on the telling nonverbal cues radiating off him.

We embrace easily, like so many times before, yet this is different. His hands linger on my hips before settling on the middle of my back. His breath holds until he blows it slowly across my neck. His eyes find my gaze like he had more to say than his voice would allow. I indulge these rare affections and give a few curve balls of my own.

"I'll miss you every day, Xander. I will never go a single moment without a thought of you. Best friend or not, you mean more to me than any other person in this world. Please be careful. I will be waiting for you." I pull away before he's able to reply. I can't stand to further delay this inevitable separation.

Xander looks down at me once more before picking up his pack and hoisting it over his shoulder. Then he tosses out the toughest blow ever dealt.

"When I am having a bad day, or we get into brutal battle,

or a friend gets hurt, or . . . just something awful happens, I will think of your smile because it always makes me happy."

Then he turns and walks toward the airline gate.

This was it. I have to tell him. It is now or never. As he passes through the threshold, I gain my courage.

"Xander!" I scream. He turns around immediately and looks startled by my outburst. It's then I realize he had planned to keep walking until I called out. I can't lay out my heart then just watch him leave.

Instead of telling him exactly how I feel, I blow him a kiss. Maybe for good luck or maybe for all the kisses I wish we had actually shared. He catches it and smiles. Then continues on his way.

Xander is much braver than I am, he's an amazing man, and he will make our country proud. But my most forefront thought is worry that I will never get to tell him how much I love him.

one

willow

Days like this are the worst. They feel like they never end. I had been on my feet since nine o'clock this morning and haven't quit. As the time nears six in the evening, I'm realizing my day needs to be done. I love my job but enough is enough.

In the past few years, I've been working as a community counselor for at-risk youth and absolutely love it. The teenagers don't always appreciate my outgoing personality but they can't constantly hide their smiles. To be considered a positive influence on these kids is extremely humbling and it brings invaluable purpose to my life.

Most of them don't have adults at home to rely on so they come to the center for the support we can offer. To think I could actually have a lasting impact on their lives is still hard to believe. Most days I feel like they are helping me more than the other way around. Their wide range of life experiences keeps my professional life far more interesting than my personal one.

Not like I can really complain about matters outside of my career. After leaving small town living for the bigger city potential, I've never looked back. I grew up in Walstrom, Minnesota and thought I would spend my life among the rolling plains where I spent my childhood. No matter how much I loved that little town, I couldn't escape the pain of *him* leaving and never returning. I had to be the one to go.

Even after all this time, thinking about him brings tears to my eyes. The broken promises, the love never reciprocated, the absolute abandonment. Xander Dixon was a huge part of my past and that is where he will always remain.

Once upon a time I thought we would get married, have a bunch of babies, and live in a cabin surrounded by the woods. We could grow old together, with nothing but one another to depend on. Our reality was much harsher than that fairytale my imagination dreamed up. I don't even know if he's still alive.

Enough about *him*. I need to stop this ridiculous obsession. Xander didn't look back while boarding that plane and it's time I walk away for good too.

Willow Shae Connor is a new woman. I don't need memories of what-might-have-been to keep me happy. Ask all my friends around Minneapolis. Just don't ask about my nonexistent love life. I'm not ready to address that.

On my way out, I swing by Lark's office to say goodbye. Since we work closely together, we formed a breezy rapport that I greatly appreciate. Our jobs can be extremely draining and it's vital to have trusted friends to process with.

I knock on her door before entering. Even after a long day, Lark is still hard at work behind her basic wood desk. She glances up as I approach and gives a slight grin. Her beautiful brown eyes give away her obvious exhaustion. This woman never quits.

"What are you still doing here? No hot date tonight?" I can't help goading her a bit.

She chuckles while rubbing her pinched forehead. "Very funny. I have piles of paperwork to get through before I even consider leaving. My head hurts just thinking about how late I'll be here."

"Dude. No way. Let's get a drink. I could really use one and clearly you need at least five. You work way too hard, Lark. If you keep pushing yourself like this, you're bound to get burnt out." I know how tough that is to hear but the truth hurts and all that.

I am all about this place but it can't be all we live for. Lark needs a serious intervention and I won't take no for an answer. She looks set to argue so I beat her to the punch.

"Seriously, let's go. Right now. You've more than earned it and that stack of stuff can wait. I'll buy the first round." I tap my foot impatiently to get her moving.

She groans loudly but pushes out of her chair. "Fine, you've talked me into it. I get to choose the place and I am ordering the most expensive drink on the menu." Her tone is full of sass but she already appears more energetic.

Score one for me. This night is definitely looking up.

———————●◆———————

A HIGH-PITCHED RING wakens me from a deep slumber. I roll over and grasp for my phone.

"Hello?' My voice is raspy from sleep.

"Oh dear, did I wake you?" My mother sounds concerned on the other end of the line.

"Hey mom. I'm up. No worries. What's going on?" I have no idea why she felt the need to call me this early on a Saturday morning.

"I just got off the phone with Meredith Dixon and she had

an interesting update on Xander that I thought you would like to know."

The mention of his name is like a punch to the gut. My heart rate instantly spikes and nerves skitter through me as I prepare for the news I'm not ready to hear yet desperate to know.

"Okay. So, how is he?" I know my voice is filled with hesitation.

"Well honey, it doesn't sound good. Meredith is very concerned. Xander has been back in the States for months but she's just now finding out. Apparently, he's gone into some sort of hiding."

"Hiding? Like he doesn't want to be found or is waiting for us to find him? I'm not sure how to take this news mom." The thought of X in any sort of pain brings instant stabs to my heart. If he is hurting, I'm hurting.

"It seems Xander went through some . . . unfortunate crud overseas and needs time for himself. No one can reach him. Xander won't talk to anyone, no matter what. Meredith isn't sure what to do."

I know my mother is stressed by the raise of her voice.

"Where is he, mom? Can we see him? I haven't talked to him in so long but I want to know he's all right."

The hitch in my mother's breath should have been my first warning. The long exhale, the next.

"When I heard Xander was back, I immediately thought of you meeting with him, but it seems he isn't interested in any reconciliation. He's isolating himself someplace up north. Meredith tried to visit but he turned her away without even opening the door." The extreme worry in her tone is evident.

"I'm not sure why you're telling me this. I haven't spoken to Xander in almost three years."

"Willow, you were the only one who could influence him when he was younger. He loved you unconditionally. The way you played together was magical. I'm not hoping for anything monumental but you could always reach that boy on a level no one else could understand." My mother's exasperated sigh told how she really felt about this situation. She wanted Xander and me to be married long ago. Unfortunately, fate had other plans.

"Mom, I'm not sure sending me out there is the right move. I've done my best to move on and I don't want to throw away the progress I've made for nothing. Yes, we were close once but not anymore. I seriously doubt he would want to see me if he wouldn't even allow his mother into the house." I wanted to scream into my pillow in exasperation with this conversation, even though it had only been a few minutes. Bringing up the past always caused a piercing pang I didn't prefer to feel.

"Would you try, Willow? For Meredith and me? If he sends you away, then at least we can say we tried. She sounds desperate for help." My mom knows I can't refuse her, especially when she is offering something I'm incredibly interested in.

"Fine, I will try to see Xander. Just let me know where he's living. I hope you know I'm agreeing to this more for you than me." The chuckle I hear through the line has me quirking an eyebrow.

"Honey, you love that boy more than a crisis patient and we both know how much you enjoy them. I appreciate you trying to contact him and I bet Meredith will be extremely grateful as well."

"Great. Thanks, mom. Text me the details and I'll let you know how it goes. Love you."

We hung up after exchanging a few more pleasantries. My heart was pounding as apprehension floods my veins at the thought of potentially visiting the boy I still love.

two

xander

I sit up in bed with a jolt. Panic seizes my limbs to the point of pain. The sheets are soaked with sweat and my hands are fisted in the blanket. Fucking nightmares never stop. I would consider myself somewhat lucky if they only plagued my dreams, but no. The suffocating torment haunts me on repeat all day and night.

What the fuck has happened to me?

Terrified was never a word I would use to describe myself but now I'm in a constant state of fear. I can't get the gruesome images and painful memories out of my head. It's like watching a tragic car crash happen over and over. There are moments when I feel a slice of relief only to get slammed with the worst thoughts. It's always pools of blood, nonstop gunshots, agonizing screams, and my brothers dying in the dirt that immediately drags me back to the day I'll never escape. Then the darkness takes over and I have to fight to breathe.

When I woke up in the hospital a year ago, I couldn't remember what happened at first. It's disgusting to admit that I wish my memory loss was permanent. Obviously, the significant damage to my body was a clue I had been involved in some serious shit, but my mind was wiped clean. I would have graciously accepted the opportunity to start over without any clue about what lurked in the recess of my mind. Life isn't quite so kind though.

When did I become such a wimpy shit?

Slowly the memories came back to me. A flicker here and a blip there, but gone in the next instant. One night I woke up screaming with vivid details replaying in my mind and it was like that opened the fucking floodgates. I went from peacefully ignorant to emotionally and mentally incapacitated in less than twenty-four hours. I was moved to a part of the hospital where my psychotic breakdowns couldn't bother other patients. I suppose that was what started my self-imposed isolation and desperate need to be alone.

The small house I'm renting is in the middle of nowhere with expansive fields surrounding it. There isn't another person around for miles in any direction and that's exactly how it should be. I need the distance from society because I don't fit in with people anymore. The windows are all boarded up and the door is locked with five deadbolts. If anyone dared to travel the rough terrain of the mile long driveway, they would assume the place has been abandoned. That's exactly what I want everyone to think.

I lost myself completely overseas and I'm not sure I'll ever recover even small pieces of who I once was. I sure as shit don't look like the guy I was years ago. If the scars covering most of my body don't alert people that I'm seriously messed up, the full beard, shaggy hair, and permanent scowl are sure to scare them off. Anyone with half a brain would take off running if they saw me headed their way.

When my mother showed up last week to visit me, I screamed the most horrifying obscenities directly in her face and watched as she slowly cowered in fear. I brutally terrified the shit out of her to ensure she wouldn't dare come back. She eventually looked at me like the monster I am, which only made me feel worse.

I am a bottomless pit of fucked up.

Even though it's the truth, and I deserve her fear, I still feel the sting from how easily she gave up. I'm such a contradictory asshole but I can't seem to find energy to do anything about it. I'm stuck in what feels like a murky hole with zero hope to escape.

Nothing can save me. The destructive corruption begins to take over my thoughts and swirls through my mind. The hate within me begins to bubble to the surface, threatening to suffocate me.

Vicious.

Dangerous.

Wretched.

Savage.

Cruel.

The venomous words are pounding into my skull.

I'm a deranged beast that deserves to fucking suffer.

Soon the flashbacks will crash down on me and drag me into the black abyss. One sure way to shut this shit up is to get wasted. So that's exactly what I do.

There is a bottle of whiskey on the counter calling my name. I stocked up on booze on my way out here. I also scheduled for some random person to drop off other necessary supplies a few times a month. I might be fucking crazy but starving to death isn't the way I want to go.

My hands are shaking as I fill a glass to the brim before guzzling it back. The liquor burns my throat but that only fuels my desire for more. I drink until the memories are fuzzy, the screams are quiet, and the images are distorted. I slam back another glass of the amber liquid for good measure.

Bile suddenly rises in my throat so I stagger to the bathroom on unstable legs. The contents of my stomach empty into the toilet bowl once my knees slam to the ground. The vomit is foul as fuck and the smell causes more puke to spew out. I gag and choke before spitting more shit out.

I'm so fucking disgusting.

After I'm done heaving my fucking guts, I wobble over to the shower. I crank the dial to the hottest setting so my blood could boil from the scorching heat. This fucked up coping mechanism seems to aggravate the demons even more but I don't give a shit. Once the steaming stream hits my numb body, I hiss in a mixture of pain and relief.

For a single moment, as I am scrubbing myself raw, it feels like the pain is washing down the drain with layers of my flesh. The scalding water burns like hell as it pelts against my weary frame but I remain standing under the spray until the temperature turns cold.

I am always fucking freezing so I didn't need to add that extreme to this psychotic torture. My abused skin feels like melted wax that is beginning to cool, which was the desired effect. I've temporarily reshaped any lingering evidence of the ghosts leering from the shadows. Maybe I could focus on the physical pain instead of the fucked up bullshit constantly racing through my mind.

I don't bother with a towel because I don't deserve the luxury. I sway on my feet before my spent limbs carry me toward the bed. Once I'm close enough, I land face first into the mattress.

The last conscious thought I have is of my buddy, in the front seat of the Humvee, smiling at me over his shoulder. Then darkness creeps into the edges of my vision before taking over completely.

three

willow

When I put the address into Google Maps, the pin appears in what looks like the middle of an open field. Strange but somewhat expected after what my mom told me. It will take over three hours to get there so I plan on this being an all day ordeal. My only hope is that Xander actually lives at this place and it isn't just a wild goose chase.

The winter weather in Minnesota is always unpredictable and of course snow started falling as soon as I left my house. My car wasn't the most reliable in these conditions and the bald tires slid along the slick highway as I increased my speed. The steering wheel shook from the effort but that could also be from my nerves.

I was desperate to reach Xander and a tiny storm wouldn't stop me. The past twenty-four hours were exasperating as I prepared for my trip. I was ready for any emergency that might come my way. I made sure the first-aid kit was in my trunk. There were extra blankets in the backseat and a bag of essential supplies rested next to me in case I got stranded.

The fluffy snowflakes transform into a blinding blast of white as I keep a steady foot on the gas pedal. The farther I traveled, the worse it got, but I refused to turn back. I was being handed an overdue opportunity to see Xander and I refused to turn back. I was intrinsically motivated to see my friend and finally find out what happened to him.

I've always been the responsible one, the caretaker, and the person others relied on in times of need. It's no surprise I went into the human services field. When Xander dropped all communication with those of us back home, I knew I would never be able to rest until I got answers.

The app alerts me that my destination is approaching on the right. Visibility is pretty minimal but I'm going slow enough that I can stop as soon as I see the house. Or so I think. Turns out the place is settled far back from the road. The only evidence of an avenue to reach it is marked by a broken post sticking straight up on one side.

The driveway is a serious challenge to navigate due to the deep layers of snow hindering my travel. By the time I reach the house, my hands are cramping from the fierce grip I've had on the steering wheel. I'm so relieved to have survived mostly unharmed that I don't pay attention to the condition of the building I am now parked in front of. Until now. There is no possible way anyone is living in there. It looks totally deserted. From the sunken roof to the dismantled porch, this shack seems beyond repair.

I didn't come all this way to just turn around upon assumption. Forcing my car door open brings a cold blast of wintery wind to freeze my face. *Lovely.* The dense powder reaches my knees when I start trudging my way to the questionable stairs. My boots sink further with each step. Not willing to take any chances, I forgo the stairs and hop directly onto the porch. From what little I can see through the cracks in the boards across the windows, it looks like all lights are off and no one is home. I give a tentative knock just to make sure.

As the door swings open, the beaming smile I had plastered on my face instantly disappears. I have to try extremely hard not to let the gasp escape past my lips. I think I succeeded but the stranger standing in front of me gives no hint one way or the other. This man is the definition of intimidating and I'm not quite sure how to handle this situation.

He's not the Xander I used to know. That much is obvious. In the three years it's been since I last saw him, he appears to have aged fifteen. The lower half of his face is covered in a thick beard, his hair has grown out and almost reaches the bottom of his ears, his shoulders appear wider than the doorframe, but it's the haunted look in his eyes that frightens me the most.

What happened to my best friend?

As I'm busy digesting these changes, I fail to notice Xander's death grip on the wood and the angry growl coming from his throat. Is he really growling? Sounds like it. Pretty sure he would have white foam coming out of his mouth if possible. This man is clearly not pleased to see me. I know he would never hurt me but I can't help feeling cautious when he's got that dangerously violent look to his stare.

Raw.

Dark.

Detached.

Yet somehow thrilling.

We are both still staring at each other, not making any movements, and I start to feel impatient. I have a horrible habit of having to always fill awkward silences and I'm scared my big mouth might cause serious issues right now. Why is he just standing there? Does he not remember me? Maybe he has memory loss . . .

Seriously, how long can this game of chicken go on? My fingers are knotted together with nervous energy while his are clenched so hard his knuckles are white. I should be the one to say something. Right? I'm clearly the idiot who showed up unannounced and obviously unwanted.

This moment revives a distant memory, from an extremely different time. When Xander and I first met, we were children. He was new in town and had wandered into the neighborhood park where I was playing. I turn my face away from this drastic contradiction to the kid I met that day. As tears build in my eyes, I let the past wash over me.

I pumped my legs faster so I could swing higher. I loved the feeling of flying, even though I was scared of heights. It was so fun to compete with my friends to find out who was the bravest. On my next downward pass, I caught sight of a boy around my age. He was alone and standing on the outer edge of the playground. He looked really sad and lonely so I decided he needed a pal.

I wasn't supposed to talk to strangers but this didn't count. I jumped off my swing and skipped over to the mysterious newcomer. He saw me coming and got a weird look on his face. Maybe he doesn't feel good. When I was standing in front of him, I stuck out my little hand to properly introduce myself.

"Hi. My name is Willow Connor and I am eight years old. What's your name?" I made sure to smile so he knew I wanted to be friends.

He stood still for a while before slipping his cool palm against mine so we could shake. I got a funny flutter in my tummy when he touched me, but it was a nice feeling, so I didn't pull away. We stared at each other without saying anything until I got antsy. I loved talking so I didn't understand why he was so quiet.

I tried again. "Do you want to play with me?" When he nodded his head and took a small step closer, I decided he was just shy. I could speak for both of us. No problem. That actually sounded really great and I decided we would be best friends.

A pleasant warmth blankets me as I recall the importance of that day. Once I dragged Xander around, explaining my favorite things, he relaxed and told me his name. Our bond seemed to form overnight and we became inseparable. I couldn't give up on him. Not then, and definitely not now.

"Xander?" I manage to squeak out. Before I can say more, he takes a step closer and, if possible, displays a more menacing look. The younger version of him fades quickly into smoke. My precious memories don't belong here.

"I thought I made it perfectly fucking clear last week by not answering the door that I want to be left the hell alone. You think I'm living out here to get bothered by anyone that randomly decides to stop in for a visit? NO! So turn the fuck around, get in your car, and LEAVE. ME. ALONE!" With that jarring roar, he steps back and slams the door with such force the whole front of the house shudders.

I'm left standing on the porch in shock. That was definitely not the way I envisioned our reunion going. The absolute devastation echoes through me as I consider what must have taken place for Xander to become the person I just saw. He was so mean and so . . . *so cold*. My friend was never rude a day in his life but this man was bitter and furious.

What happened?

With no other choice, I turn around to leave. The snow is falling even harder now as I stumble back to my car. There is no way I'm getting out of this driveway but I don't want to risk another encounter with that behemoth of a man. I'll sleep in my car if I have to. I don't think Xander took the time to notice how many inches were already covering the ground. I don't think he noticed much of anything at all.

four

xander

After I slam the door, I hurl my body against it out of frustration before sliding down to the floor. I bang my head against the wood because I'm still in shock over what just happened. What the fuck was she doing here? After all these years, I never expected her to just show up like we were still friends. That's fucking laughable.

I haven't had a friend since they all got blown up and I was left to survive in this world alone. That's my punishment and I own that shit. They're all dead. Gone in an instant. Buried in the cold ground. Never to breathe precious air into their lungs again. I can't even pay tribute to their lives without having a fucking meltdown. I'm such a freak.

I don't deserve to be cared about when they all had that privilege brutally stolen away from them. I'll be secluded the rest of my miserable life and I won't expect anything more. I have confined myself to solitude out here to suffer in silence. I don't need anyone checking up on me like I'm some invalid.

I will never allow anyone to offer me comfort or relief from the hell I'm trapped in. The depressing loneliness only exacerbates my misery and reality is slipping further away each day I remain in solitude. I don't know how fucking long I can survive without giving a shit. I can't fucking accept these opposing existences clashing together.

I bash my head back against the thick door again, just to feel the pain. When I get started down this ugly path, it is almost impossible to stop the rage and panic from taking over. I'm such a fucking pussy. Getting all bent out of shape because *she* showed up. I thought today was going to be decent.

I know I should be thankful to be alive, to still feel my heart beating in my chest, but I don't feel so lucky. I'm haunted by the horrific images of my comrades dying, the bombs blasting through the air, the screams of innocent lives ending well before their time. That shit will stick with me for the rest of my life, as it should. The wrong guys died that day and I would have gladly taken their place.

I'm ashamed that the sole survivor of my entire troop has turned into this sniveling idiot. I'm a disgrace to their memory and I can't seem to do a damn thing about it. I can't even have a conversation with my mother or my best friend.

It's so fucking strange that Willow popped up out of nowhere. Her unexpected presence brings a lot of conflicted confusion that I really can't handle. I already think about her far too often but suddenly she appeared, like a fucking ghost from my past. I could almost trick myself into believing the vision of her was another hallucination, but I couldn't replicate her level of perfection. Willow's enticing scent assaulted me and left my mouth fucking watering. I almost reached out to stroke her porcelain cheek until I remembered the fucking repercussions that touch would bring.

Her silky brown hair looked black against the blizzard backdrop. Her emerald irises were sparkling with mischief and curiosity, but more was hidden in their depths. If I really wanted to waste time analyzing pointless shit, I could convince myself there was love swirling in her captivating greens.

She was fucking gorgeous.

Seeing Willow again is like taking a direct hit to my chest. I loved that girl with all I had to give but never did a damn thing about it. She was always so pure and bright. What could she ever see in a loser like me? I wanted to make something of myself so I had more to offer her. I wanted to be a man she would be proud to claim.

The fantasy of us getting hitched and having a fleet of children when I was done with my tour had kept me company. I often dreamed of it on those long, lonely nights. Too bad I was always too chicken shit to tell her my feelings and now she will never know. Fuck, I missed her something fierce but I couldn't even talk to her when she showed up at the door. I just pushed her away and hid behind my bullshit armor.

My head falls into my hands and then I yank on my hair. What the fuck have I done? The one chance I get to speak to Willow and I act like a demented moron. She sure as hell won't be coming back. I made sure of that, just like with my mother. No point dwelling on it. Not like she would want anything to do with me once she realized what I've become. I'm sure she kicked up rocks with how fast she tore out of here.

I slowly stand and stretch before securing all the locks. When I glance out the window, I'm shocked to see a car in my driveway. Why is Willow still here? With a closer look, it seems her tires are spinning in the thick snow that now covers the ground. She keeps trying to move forward, which is only making the ruts she's stuck in worse. Willow is not going anywhere anytime soon if she keeps that up.

Whether I like it or not, I'm going to have to go out there to help her. How can I do that without speaking to her?

I can't believe this shit.

It looks like I'll get another chance after all. How quickly can I fuck it up this time?

five

willow

"Crap!" I yell out and slam my palms against the steering wheel. Even in this unfortunate situation, I can't force an actual swear word past my lips. I blow out a heavy exhale before resting my head on my arm. I need to get out of here before Xander finds me lingering on his property. I can't even imagine his reaction.

My rear tires keep spinning as I slam on the gas again, hoping to actually gain traction this time.

Gosh, dang it! What am I supposed to do?

I grab my cell but since I'm apparently on the set of a low budget horror film, it has no reception. At least I was smart enough to pack a charger. I would laugh at the ridiculous cliché if I wasn't the one stuck out here. I gnaw on my lip as the worry materializes and intensifies.

With one glance out the window, I know it's a terrible idea

to attempt hiking to the road in order to catch a signal. I wouldn't make it. I can hardly see a few feet in front of me, let alone the end of the driveway. It's also starting to get dark, which only adds to the nightmare backdrop.

I'm trapped out here in the middle of freaking nowhere. This place is surrounded by open fields on one side and dense forest on the other. So yeah, I'm totally stranded with no hope of rescue. Who comes to plow the massive driveway in situations like this?

That stranger locked inside the house isn't going to help me. *Just my luck.* This is what I get for trying to be caring and compassionate. I can't forget curious. It's the last one that always gets me into these messes. My friends would be laughing their butts off at my internal shaming right now.

A loud bang on the trunk of my car causes a high-pitched scream to rush out of my throat. Why is all this scary stuff happening to me at once? I bump my head on the window and nearly have a heart attack as I try to assess the threat.

What the heck?

I whip around in my seat and see the reason for my panic. Xander, in all his hulking glory, is glowering at me from behind my vehicle. He's looking at me like I'm responsible for some serious crime by just sitting here. I almost wiggle my fingers at him in a patronizing wave.

Am I supposed to get out? What does he expect me to do? He must have noticed me spinning out. I'm clearly not going anywhere, anytime soon. He can't possibly expect me to walk home.

Even though I'm a bit distracted by my mental musing, I can still make out the yell from outside.

"Get in the house!" Xander growls out, accompanied by another solid pound to my trunk.

He's going to let me into his place? I didn't expect that at all. Maybe this will give us an opportunity to actually talk. Opening my door takes serious effort but I manage when I throw my whole body into the action. Of course this also causes me to tumble out into the snow. Can I get a freaking break?

I lay there for a moment, basking in my embarrassment, waiting to see if Xander will offer me a hand. I don't hear any movement so I tip my head back to make sure. Just as I figured. The butthead is still standing in the exact same spot with the scowl still firmly on his lips.

I make sure to groan extra loud while awkwardly rolling over, followed by ungracefully standing up. I almost want to take a bow because this whole situation is so ridiculous. Once I'm back on my two feet, I make a big production of brushing all the white fluff off my clothes. Still no reaction from the big guy. I'm seriously beginning to wonder if there is something wrong with his brain function.

"Get in the house. I'll stay in the shack," Xander grumbles out and jerks his chin in the direction I'm assuming he plans to go. Considering the condition of his home, I'm beyond concerned at what shape the other building is in for him to refer to it as a shack. We might not be friends anymore but I still care about the man.

"Can't we stay in there together?" I question. I'm not ashamed to admit I'm scared to be in his place alone on top of the worry he's holing up someplace even more rundown. His response is immediate.

"No." That's it. Just no. It would be a waste of breath arguing. I've quickly figured that out in the short time we've . . . talked, if you could call it that.

Xander turns and heads toward the forest side of his property. I quickly lose sight of him since the flurries are casting a white hue and wreaking havoc on my vision. Just in case he's still within hearing range, I decide to give him some gratitude. "Great! Thank you so very much, Xander. You've been really helpful!" I scream out into the wind.

What a jerk.

I begin the journey back to the porch I stood on not even an hour ago. My previous tracks aren't covered completely so I'm able to use them to make the trek easier. I bypass the stairs once again then carefully use the railing to kick the snow off my boots. Getting a self-guided tour of Xander's home should be mighty interesting.

I just hope he didn't lock the door.

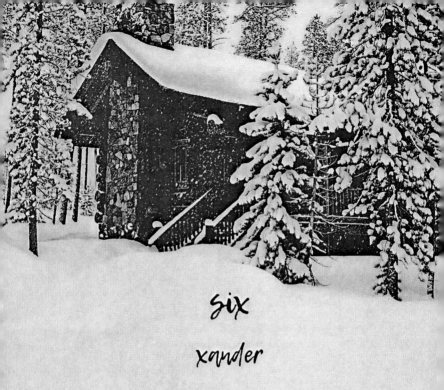

six

xander

What the fuck was I thinking offering to let Willow stay in my house? Not only is that a huge invasion of the carefully constructed privacy I have built, but now I'm stuck sleeping out in the shed. At least there is a blanket stashed in here. Not like it would really matter. No way in hell am I going back in my home with Willow violating the space.

I couldn't let her sleep out in her car. I might be an asshole but even I have some manners left. That thought reminds me of when Willow fell into the snow. *Still a klutz.* It took all my control not to laugh at her flailing about. When was the last time I even smiled?

Willow is making dents to my damaged exterior without even trying. In a twisted way, I feel almost relieved to have her stomping all over my mangled layers. She's proving to me that I'm not completely dead inside. Even though I would never admit it,

I feel a tiny sliver of light mixing in with all the darkness.

When I first opened the door and saw her standing there, I had this small sense of relief crash into me. It overpowered the anger constantly pulsing through me. I actually had to work hard to keep my expression detached and unfazed. What the fuck is up with that?

It doesn't hurt that she's so damn hot. Willow had always been a pretty girl and had plenty of boys drooling at her feet. I followed her around like a love-struck fool. Her vibrant green gaze could stare so deep I thought she could see all my lewd thoughts. Her pouty lips could get me to do anything she asked. I always imagined running my fingers through her long raven hair. Willow would release a breathy sigh and whisper out my name.

I'm more than shocked to find my visual stroll-down-adolescent-lane has caused a physical reaction. I'm rock fucking hard. I can't even remember the last time I was turned on.

Holy shit.

Bringing my fantasy into the present, I imagine Willow walking into my house. I can't help wondering what she's doing right now. Even all bundled up, I can tell she has a body made for sin. All curves and smooth lines. I bet the first thing she did was slowly unzip her coat to reveal a skin-tight sweater that hugs her body like a second skin. She catches my gaze and untamed lust causes her irises to expand. She looks hungry as she begins to stalk towards me. I would gladly be her next meal.

I yank my pants down enough to expose my dick and hiss as the cold air stings my sensitive flesh. My fingers barely touch when I wrap my palm around it because I'm that fucking hard. I haven't jerked off since before the ambush and I know this won't take long. Especially with seductive visions of Willow filtering through my imagination.

Her fingers rake through her long hair before sliding down her torso. Willow grabs the bottom edge of her shirt then eases it up so slowly it's agonizing. Her stomach is toned and flat. Her generous rack pushed up by a lacy fuck-me bra. Her slender neck stretched back as the sweater goes over her head. With each new sliver of exposed skin, my cock grows impossibly stiffer.

My fist starts a slow glide, with a tight grip, just to get used to the sensation. Prickles creep up my spine as my hand strokes faster and I refocus on my erotic illusion. My balls are already beginning to tighten and Willow is still half dressed.

I picture Willow unsnapping her bra before slowly sliding the straps down her shoulders. She's taking slow, measured steps toward me as she sets her tits free with a magnificent bounce. Her nipples are stunned by the frosty air and instantly harden into stiff peaks. I'm so mesmerized by her voluptuous breasts that I don't notice her beginning to lower her leggings.

I groan loudly as the pleasure courses through my limbs. The pressure in my fucking dick is close to exploding but I hold back a bit longer. Willow is busy pushing her pants down and enticing me further by giving an extra swing to her hips. The sight of her like this is driving me crazier than I already am.

The only thing left is that tiny strip of fabric between her legs. Her mouth curves into a coy smile as she hooks her fingers into the sides. Her tongue peeks out and slowly licks along her puffy bottom lip as the panties drop to the floor. Fuck me, she's stunning. The image my mind is conjuring up of Willow is completely captivating me, seducing me.

What would happen if she was actually standing in front of me?

A rumble tears from my mouth as I yank myself even harder, almost to the point of pain. The sexy temptress sashays into the bathroom. She bends slowly, giving me a tantalizing view of her delectable ass, and turns on the shower. The steam billows out around her, which gives the room a heavenly effect. A halo seems to appear on Willow's head.

My Angel.

The tendrils of hate and shame are trying to pull me back from the edge. I don't deserve to experience an ounce of pleasure after abandoning my brothers. The familiar stab of pain floods my system with an image of them bleeding out. They reach for me with broken limbs and cry out for help. Their searching fingers morph into a lethal noose tightening around my neck, attempting to rob the air from my lungs. I choke as my free hand goes to my throat while my occupied palm continues the punishing strokes. The darkness is thick but my eyes rapidly scan for any sight of light.

A bright shimmer forms in front of me and I use all my strength to focus on that tiny spot. My fucking mind is playing nasty tricks on me but for once, I regain control and the poison ricochets off me.

I am once again lost to the images of Willow naked, in the shower, with water streaming down her perfect body. Her skin glows from the sunlight streaming in. I want to reach out and caress every delectable inch. I want to run my tongue along every delicious inch.

She glances over her shoulder with a shy smile gracing her lips. That look is reserved just for me and that's what tosses me over into oblivion. My balls tighten as my cock throbs with release. The orgasm feels ripped out of me and is so intense that my back arches at a painful angle. My cum fills my palm and spills over as I continue stroking through the pleasure. It seems endless and I'm suspended in a bewildered state. Eventually my withered body collapses to the floor, totally spent. My hand is still grasping my softening dick as I picture Willow blowing me a kiss.

For the first time in years, I drift off to sleep with a clear mind as a calming sensation settles over me. I'll allow the guilt to catch up with me tomorrow.

seven

willow

I'm startled awake by what sounds like a tree collapsing right by my head. I blink my tired eyes several times before taking in my surroundings. It only takes a quick moment for me to recall where I am and that I slept in Xander's bed. His mattress is huge and smells so delicious, I want to roll around in the sheets in hopes that the scent will cling to me.

My mischievous thoughts are rudely interrupted by another loud THWACK.

Seriously, what is that?

My curiosity gets the best of me once again and instead of spending more time in this pillowy fortress, I roll to the edge and slide my feet to the floor. I stretch my stiff limbs before padding over to the covered window. When I lean over to take a peek through a crack in the boards, I almost fall over at the sight before me.

Xander is all I can see. It's like an extreme case of tunnel vision.

Holy cow!

He looks so sexy in a plain gray shirt and faded jeans. His dark unruly hair is covered by a black beanie but my attention doesn't linger there long. My eyes quickly scan back to his torso and the obviously damp fabric clinging to flexing muscles.

Wow.

I mean, yeah, wow.

Xander is freaking ripped.

My hands press against the rough wood as I very audibly gulp down the saliva that had been prepared to dribble down my chin. This is serious lady porn and I am not ashamed to admit it. An erotic vision filters into my conscious and the fantasy of Xander making me his, in every way possible, takes over.

First he needs to ditch that freaking shirt.

If Xander took off that soaking fabric to expose his sculpted abs and bulging biceps, I might spontaneously combust right here. Even without his muscles directly showing, my body flushes with an embarrassing level of arousal. I am extremely turned on by this man.

As I continue creeping like a stalker, I notice for the first time what Xander is doing. All that noise is from him splitting wood. He is confident and capable with the large axe in his hands. Xander must spend a lot of time cutting up trees and his body is *very* solid proof of his hard work.

Xander sets another log up before swinging the axe down in a sharp arc to split it perfectly down the center. The resounding *thwack* echoes through the trees and I swear it makes the wood beneath my hands vibrate. I watch him repeat this action over and over until I feel embarrassed for leering at him without his knowledge.

I turn away from the window and glance around the rest of

the house. Calling this place a house is actually quite generous. It is definitely more of a cabin and needs serious remodeling. When I came in last night, I couldn't see much but I could instantly tell the inside matched the crumbling exterior. It looks even more depressing in the light of day.

The walls are all bare and free of any decorations. There are mismatched pieces of furniture strewn about that look older than my mother. The kitchen is tiny and equipped for only the most basic tasks. The fireplace is a monstrosity and more of an eyesore than anything. I suppose it has the purpose of heating this place up but based off the chill in the air, probably needs to be replaced as well. For now, it couldn't hurt to add another log to the glowing embers.

Xander's bed is the focal point in the entire room and clearly the only thing he took time to pick out. Priorities and all that. I get distracted for a moment imagining his bulky body sprawled out on the unmade sheets. I bet his defined form would look mighty fine lying there. Too bad I'll never get to witness it. He can't seem to handle being around me for more than a few minutes without fleeing one way or another.

The hopelessness crashes down on me and I want to collapse under the overwhelming weight.

What am I doing here?

I've been trying to resurrect a connection that has been severed for too long. Xander claims he wants to be left alone but I've accidently managed to disrupt his solitude. Technically, it isn't my fault that I'm stuck here but he clearly doesn't see it that way.

Now I'm surrounded by his meager belongings after spying on his lumberjack routine. I need to get control over my wacky libido and put thoughts of banging Xander to rest. It's definitely not going to happen.

I recall giving myself a very similar speech years ago. The occasion was vastly different but the topic was eerily familiar.

Wasn't senior prom meant to be a night to remember? If that was the case, I was being seriously let down.

First of all, my date was not the guy I wanted to be with. Dave was fine but that was part of the issue. He didn't give me butterflies or cause me to daydream about our future wedding. Dave was a substitute for the real deal, who happened to be dancing with another girl a few feet away.

Xander was slowly swaying to the music with Angela snuggled in his arms. Lucky freaking duck. She was clinging to him like a second layer of skin and it drove me bananas. All I could think about was dragging her away by that mop of poorly bleached hair. Gross.

Obviously, I was crazed with jealousy. Not that Xander would ever know. He wanted to be just friends with me so he could date a bimbo like Angela. I was getting pretty sick of watching their little display of inappropriate affection. Wasn't there a rule about how much space there should be between dance partners?

Dave squeezed my palm, which reminded me I'm being extremely rude by completely ignoring him. When I glimpsed up at him, he smiled and I felt even worse. I should try harder with him. He's a nice, dependable guy. A little boring but that's all right. Urgh. Even thinking about it made me lose interest.

Dave moved closer to my side before speaking. "I'm going to grab a soda. Do you want anything?"

I shook my head and he walked off toward the coolers. My attention refocused on the happy couple still squished together. Thankfully my groan was drowned out by the music. Even though I'm positive he couldn't have heard me, Xander snapped his head in my direction.

When he noticed I was alone, he untangled Angela from his body before strolling toward me. A lazy grin lifted one side of his perfect mouth and I got a little light headed from the visual impact.

As Xander approaches, I got a whiff of his trademark scent and had to clamp my jaw so a moan doesn't break free. I couldn't handle this much longer. He wrapped a muscular arm around my shoulder before whispering, "Why are you standing over here alone, Wills?"

I instinctively melted into him before responding. "Dave is getting something to drink." I jerked my chin in the direction he went. Xander glanced over his shoulder before invading me with a serious blue-eyed stare.

Upon hearing my date's name, I swore Xander's eyes flashed with something possessive, but that can't be right. His growly tone increased my suspicions though. "I still can't believe you're here with him. Seriously, Willow? What do you see in him?"

My defensive hackles rose. "You're really one to talk, X. Should we talk about your new girlfriend over there? She looks ready to slit my throat based off that death glare she's sporting." I chuckled in annoyance as my frustration made my stomach churn. Maybe I should just go home.

Before I can make a move for the door, Xander yanked me onto the makeshift dance floor. In the next moment, I'm enveloped in his embrace as we start a smooth rhythm. I rested my head on his chest and released a heavy sigh.

"Angela isn't my girlfriend." I could barely hear him, but I made out his grunted words. I angled my face up so I could hear him better. "You could have fooled me."

"Don't be crazy, Wills. You know I wouldn't date a girl like her."

"So you're just screwing her?" I felt my anger rising again.

Of course Xander picked up on my mood. "What's your deal? This is supposed to be a fun night."

"I'm crabby and Dave is dull. Being with you is the highlight of my evening." I realized too late how that last part could be interpreted.

Xander closed the distance between us so our foreheads touched. Our breath exchanged in the small gap separating our mouths. If I shifted forward a bit, we would be kissing. It seemed like Xander had a similar thought because his ocean irises flashed with awareness. He inched closer and my inaudible gasp escaped. He must have felt my reaction being pressed together so close.

"I love spending time with you too, Wills."

Our almost-kiss fades into the past where it belongs as I

flop down into the nearby chair. Reminiscing about Xander be-ing sweet is not helping my case and I need to knock it off. The sooner I can get out of here the better, but there is no way my car is moving without an intervention.

I can still hear the resounding *thwack* as Xander chops away while I finish perusing the cabin's bleak atmosphere. I heave out a heavy sigh as I consider my options. What am I supposed to do now?

eight

xander

I've been awake since dawn cutting up a tree that fell from the storm last night. Thankfully the weather cleared up so I could get some work done. Splitting wood is one of the only ways I can get my mind to shut down for a while. The repetitive motions of the menial task keep me occupied enough to quiet the chaos lurking inside. With the first swing of my axe, I can feel my thoughts calm and I easily settle into an effortless rhythm.

After pushing my body for hours, I am soaked with sweat and utterly exhausted. Usually I would keep going until I couldn't move but today there is a certain someone distracting me from going that far.

How in the hell am I supposed to face Willow after what I did last night? I'm such a pervert. It had already taken all my energy to maintain eye contact with her before I blew my load all over the shack. Now I'm going to come off as an even bigger jackass when I can't even look at her.

Why do I care?

She's all alone in my house. Looking at my stuff, touching everything, and silently judging who I've become in her absence. She's letting her intoxicating scent seep into my private space. Willow is destroying the secretive existence that I've carefully built around myself. I'm too much of a fucking coward to admit I like it.

A whole hell of a lot.

I can't help the growl that tears up my throat.

How did this fucking happen?

Why the fuck couldn't she just leave me alone?

I don't want her here, dammit!

I clench my hands into fists and bang them on my head.

Why do I have to be so fucked up?

I can't let the darkness pull me under with Willow so close. She already thinks I'm screwed up enough as it is. I'm panting out hefty breaths that come out looking like plumes of smoke. Being a Minnesota native comes in handy with these freezing winters.

Since moving back, I've discovered that I enjoy the extreme temperature more than I ever remember. Feeling the frigid air bite into my heated skin is a stark relief. As the chill slowly soaks in, it complements the cold I always feel deep inside.

When I turn toward the house, I wonder what Willow is doing in there. I don't have a lot of shit to occupy her but that girl can be entertained with a strand of yarn. It always surprised me that she could find fun in any random thing.

Maybe she's still sleeping though, calm and compliant. I easily imagine her naked in my bed, touching herself under the covers. Taunting me with her seductive movements.

With that enticing vision flooding my mind, a memory slams into me from my previous life. Before all this shit ruined me.

I close my eyes and let the past consume me.

Going to the beach was a great way to spend a hot summer day.

Witnessing Willow in a skimpy bikini was a fine sight and I always took advantage of the opportunity. Even if it was the worst type of torture. All look but absolutely no touch. It fucking sucked.

I'd been lusting after this girl for years but I'd been friend-zoned hardcore. It doesn't help that I'd never made a move.

Willow was sprawled out on a towel next to me and I swore she was trying to kill me with what she's wearing. Or not wearing, I should say. How is that scrap of fabric considered a swimsuit?

Practically all of her silky skin was golden from the sun and on display for everyone to see. I was going crazy trying to restrain myself from running my tongue along her toned stomach. Then gliding my fingers under the tiny triangle cups covering her plump tits. My palm was itching to feel how smooth her thigh was.

Her body was what kept wet dreams in business. Trust me, I would know.

It was weird as hell to be picturing her naked when we were sitting there, just lounging on the beach. But we seemed to be just something all the time, nothing more.

Just hanging out.

Just friends.

Just bullshit.

She gave me a shy smile and I almost creamed my fucking shorts. I bit the shit out of my cheek to keep it locked down. My dirty mind is bad enough. I don't need to pop a stiffy and raise all sorts of speculations.

Damn though. My best friend was fine as hell.

Maybe I'd own up to my feelings and actually do something about them. Not today, but I damn well wished for it one day. Maybe soon.

I was such a wimp.

I shake off the adolescent daydream and can almost laugh at the irony. I'm still fucking chicken shit. I guess everything hasn't changed.

I need to let go of this stupid ray of hope I seem to be holding onto. Willow and I will never be together. It didn't happen back then and it sure as fuck isn't happening now.

When I blink to clear my eyes, I try to rein in my emotional crap and get control of myself. I really need to stop fucking obsessing over her. That woman will be gone soon enough and I will be back to my isolated reality. Having her here was nothing more than a tiny blip on the radar. Getting rid of her is exactly what I want.

I rub at the sudden ache in my chest and wonder if all the drinking is starting to catch up to me. Might have something to do with the fact that I haven't eaten anything yet. Getting food involves going in the house though and I'm not sure I can handle seeing Willow quite yet.

I'm such a fucking pussy.

She's the one invading my place so there is no reason for me to be cowering outside. That damn dream is still swirling through my head and fucking with my mind. The visions were so vivid and felt so real that I'm getting half hard reminiscing.

I just need to ignore Willow and push her out the door. With that brilliant plan in place, I step onto the covered path that leads to the front porch so I can evict my unwanted guest.

nine

willow

The door swings open without warning and bangs against the wall. I yelp out in surprise and knock over the chair beside me. This man has the worst habit of disrupting the freaking peace with his rude behavior. He doesn't need to barbarically barge in and scare the crap out of me. *Again.*

"You didn't lock the fucking deadbolt?!" Xander roars out from the entrance of the room. Someone obviously woke up on the wrong side of the shack.

Why is he so darn grumpy?

I can't help remembering how sexy this jerk looked earlier. Even though he's yelling at me for no reason. Xander is wearing the same shirt and from this distance, I can definitely see the ripple of hard abs.

Dang, he's so freaking hot.

Am I drooling for real this time? Maybe he could help me

out and let me borrow his shirt to wipe my mouth. Then I could get a peek at what Xander is hiding under there.

Shoot! I totally zoned out imagining him stripping off that unnecessary material. Did he say something about locking the deadbolt? Xander sure looks like he's waiting for me to respond. His glare and snarl suggest his patience is already thin. I take a shot in the dark.

"Umm, why would I lock the door? Do you get a lot of unwanted visitors I need protecting from? I figured it was pretty safe considering we're in the middle of nowhere," I reply with extra sass in my tone.

Who does this guy think he is?

I know I let him intimidate me before but I woke up this morning with newfound courage. He can't keep pushing me around without expecting consequences eventually. He seems to forget we used to be best friends and I know how to defend myself. I'll get my freaking way, it just might take longer than I originally anticipated.

Xander is gritting his teeth and flexing his fingers, not moving any closer to me. "That's the kind of stupid thinking that will get your ass in trouble," he spits out.

I'm so done with this conversation. Clearly this isn't the chance I've been waiting years for. He can't see anything passed his stubborn agenda to get rid of me. I'll make a quick call and get out of this senseless ordeal. I should have never come out here without getting more information.

"I need to use your phone so I can get someone to tow my car out of your driveway. I have no cell reception. I'm sure my mom is worried sick about me by this point." I try to keep my voice as even and calm as possible.

"Does it look like I have a damn phone?" Xander sneers out.

Geesh, he's so angry.

I'll never understand what caused all that hostility to bottle up inside him.

"Well, how am I supposed to call my mom then?" I question lightly, doing my best to ease him out of his temper tantrum.

He snorts loudly while crossing his massive arms across his chest. "Not my problem."

Never one to mince words.

This nasty attitude has his face contorting into an awful mask and enough is enough. "Why are you such a jerk? I didn't purposely get stuck in your driveway. I'm not trying to disrupt whatever warped paradise you've created for yourself out here. I want to leave. *Trust me.* But since I can't, I need your help. I will gladly get out of your space as soon as I can get someone to pick me up."

Halfway through my babbling, Xander arches one eyebrow. Otherwise, there is no sign of emotion on his face. His mouth sets into a grim line I'm starting to recognize in the short time I've been around. His once deeply soulful eyes are now blank. He just seems so expressionless and it bothers me more than I can handle. I need to get used to this new side of Xander but I feel my heart ache all over again. My entire being is weighed down with disappointment that I can't get him to budge. Just an inch.

Before he can spew more venom my way, I decide to just leave. I can walk to the road and try to make a call from there. I will do whatever it takes to get away from this stranger.

"Forget it. I'll figure it out on my own," I wheeze out as I sneak past him and out the door.

I will not cry, dang it!

He's not worth getting so upset over.

Even though I try to hold them back, I feel the first tears trickle down my cheeks. I angrily wipe them away, rougher than necessary, as I continue marching toward my car for my phone. Now that the weather has cleared up, I can see the huge rut my vehicle seems to be nestled in. There is no way I'm getting out of that without assistance. I can barely get the door open.

I snag my cell off the charger before slamming the door closed. The snow has to be at least eight inches deep, which makes walking an extreme chore. My muscles already ache from the additional exertion. It's also pretty dang cold outside, which doesn't help my already foul mood. The tears are coming faster now and I've lost the motivation to swipe the streaks away.

Freaking Xander and his wretched demeanor. I can empathize with him to a certain extent because I'm sure what he experienced overseas must have been horrendous. There is a limit to the amount of crap I will put up with though. I was willing and more than ready to be his friend again. Provide any support he might need and be a stable shoulder to lean on. Clearly Xander wants nothing to do with me or any sympathy I was willing to provide.

I shouldn't care so much. He was gone for three years and I got used to living without him.

Even as I think it, I know that's a total lie. I never got over his abandonment. It ate at me, festering and growing, every day, until he miraculously showed back up. Xander isn't the only one who has changed. I didn't know how impacted I was by his absence until I stood facing him yesterday.

Perhaps on the exterior I seemed calm, but inside I was freaking out. My stomach has been tied in painful knots while my mind bounces between emotions. It all just slammed into me at once and the misery was the most overwhelming. Especially witnessing his tormented transformation.

I keep stumbling along, fighting with my thoughts the entire time. I'm about halfway when my phone starts going berserk in my hand. I've apparently hit a sweet spot so I better take advantage. I quickly clear all the notifications I just received to dial my mom's number. I really hope she's home and my dad can come help me right away.

After a single ring, my mother's frantic voice answers.

"Willow? Oh my goodness, please tell me you're alright." Her genuine worry and obvious care helps soothe some of the pain Xander has caused over the last twenty-four hours.

"Hi mom. I'm fine, mostly. I'm so glad you picked up. I need dad to come out here with his plow so I can get my car out. It's practically buried in the snow." I can't keep the sniffle out of my voice even though I know it will only ratchet her concern up higher.

"Sweetie, what on earth has you so upset? Is it Xander? What happened?" Her insistent questioning seems relentless but I can't handle giving her the details in my current emotional state.

"Mom, please, I can't talk about it now. Can dad come out here?" I push out. My throat is tightening from holding back the cry wanting to escape.

"Willow, you're really scaring me. Your father is still on the road from his last job site down in Rochester. He won't be home until later tonight. I'm sorry, darling," she coos.

That was not what I wanted to hear and my mood plummets impossibly further. "Crud. Alright. Can you come get me right away? Could you do that, please? We'll have to come back for my car, I guess. I'll tell you everything when you get here." I'm trying so hard not to openly sob but I'm losing the battle quickly.

"Of course, Willow. I can be there in an hour, if I remember correctly when I looked up the address before. Are you safe until then?" My mom's question makes me wonder where I can wait for her. I guess I can sit in my car. I'm definitely not planning to face Xander again.

"Thank you so much, Mom. Seriously, I owe you. I'll be waiting in my car. I don't have reception closer to Xander's house so you won't be able to call me. I'll be watching for you and meet you at the road. Don't try to pull into the driveway. I'll see you soon, okay?" I'm sure the relief is evident in my voice with my reply. I would love to chat with her longer but I'm freezing standing out here.

"I already have my coat on, Sweetie. I'll be there as soon as I can. I expect a lot of answers, Willow Shae," she chides me with that last remark. I'll tell her every last detail if that makes her get here faster.

"See you soon, Mom. Thanks again," I respond while turning back toward my car. I wait for her farewell before hanging up.

The trek back isn't as tough because I managed to make a decent path on my way out here. I keep my head down to keep the chill away. I scrub at my cheeks to remove the frozen crystals my tears turned into. With the knowledge that my mom is coming to get me, I feel marginally better. I'm able to focus on my rescue and try to move past everything that happened with Xander.

Once I get settled in my car and it's starting to warm up, I think of the best way I can pass the time. I suppose I could read a few chapters of the sexy romance I started last week. I'm not really in the mood though. I can't seem to help the quick peek I take of Xander's house in front of me. I really wish I hadn't because he's standing in the open doorway shooting daggers with his eyes. It appears that my car is his intended target. If looks could cause damage, all my tires would be flat.

Xander storms toward me when he notices me turned around in my seat looking at him. Just super. I really didn't want to have another altercation with him.

He yanks open my door with so much force I'm surprised it's still attached and didn't rip off the hinges. Xander starts barking questions at me as soon as the barrier between us is gone.

"What are you doing?"

"Leave me alone, Xander."

"Why are you just sitting out here?"

"I'm waiting for my ride."

"Who's coming?"

"Like that's any of your business."

His eyes flash with irritation. He has no right to expect answers from me. He's been nothing but cruel and rude. Xander is looming over me and he has an even greater size advantage with me sitting down.

"I deserve to know who's planning to step foot on my property, Willow." His hands are clenched in tight fists and I notice a slight tremble. Xander appears extremely bothered by the idea of another person being here and I should have realized that. I rely on my trauma training to assess this situation more clearly. Xander isn't isolating himself out here for no reason. I feel really guilty for potentially pushing him into a panic.

I ease out of the car so I can stand facing him. I want to be on more common ground when I apologize. I reach out and gently place my hand on his forearm.

"Listen Xander–" but before I can say more, he rips his arm away and stumbles back. He has a lost look in his eyes that makes me feel even worse. Until he opens his mouth.

"Don't fucking touch me!" He grits out as he continues backing away from me. I'm instantly wounded and offended by his reaction. I try not to take it personally since it's obvious Xander is dealing with some serious issues. I really attempt to keep a straight face but I feel my bottom lip wobble beyond my control. My eyes flood and tears spill over before I can hide the evidence of my pain. I can't believe how different he is.

"I'm sorry, Xander. *For everything.* I never should have come. It's clear you don't want to be bothered. I'll wait for my ride near the road. Take care of yourself," I hush out, trying to keep my voice even. I grab my stuff from the car before taking a last look at my former best friend. He hasn't moved but his entire body is shaking.

What happened to him?

That worrying thought keeps my mind occupied as I make the hike to wait for my mom.

ten

xander

As I watch Willow trudge away, I feel like a worthless piece of shit that can't do anything fucking right. My mood seems to get progressively worse with each step she takes. I can't escape the brick of regret lodged in my chest. If I wasn't such a fuckup, I would go after her. I could potentially fix the disturbing impression she has of me. When I can no longer see her from where I stand, I feel the darkness begin to descend upon me.

I can't believe I almost lost my shit in front of her. She was seriously testing my already short fucking fuse when she wouldn't tell me who was picking her up. Then she had to touch me. The pain that flashed across Willow's face at my reaction made me feel like such an asshole. I could have tried explaining my response if I hadn't been using all of my energy to stop the looming meltdown.

What could I have possibly said to make it any fucking better?

To make matters even more confusing, I didn't feel the typical repulsiveness when Willow's hand made contact with my skin. I yanked my arm away out of pure instinct rather than the searing pain that causes my reaction. I was shocked to find it didn't hurt. Before I could explain anything, Willow mumbled out a completely unnecessary apology and started walking away. If anyone has stuff to be sorry for, it's my messed up ass.

I can't stand being touched. It feels like acid is burning my flesh then slowly ripping away from the bone. The doctors couldn't explain the sudden onset. I refused to sit through any head shrinking sessions where they would conclude I was fucked up beyond repair. I already knew all that shit. They ended up tossing it in with all the other trauma symptoms I was suffering from. It wasn't like I planned to be around people so what did it matter.

The more I reflect on it, the more I realize Willow's touch was actually soothing. For one short moment, I felt a breath of peace. Then I went and fucked it all up because that's what I do. Nothing good happens to me and I need to fucking accept it, even if Willow tries blasting her blinding light into the depths of my darkness.

Her unexpected presence disrupted the warped routine I was used to but now I'll slink back into the abyss. There is no escape from this distorted existence I'm suffocating in. I don't deserve any reprieve from the constant battle waging war inside my head.

Why am I still standing here? Why am I obsessing over this?

With that thought, I turn back to my house to retreat into my reality. When I try to step forward, it feels like I'm pushing against an armored wall. Almost like my feet are cemented to the ground. I have officially gone insane. I grit my teeth and plow through the invisible force field attempting to hold me captive.

The first thing I do once I get back inside is rip all the sheets off the bed. I can't have any reminders of Willow lingering around. With the fabric crumpled in my fists, I lurch back when her scent reaches my nostrils. The distinct lavender aroma screams her name. It forces memories of countless occasions I breathed the exact perfume deep into my lungs whenever I was near her.

It smells so fucking good.

I'm powerless against the desire to inhale more of the intoxicating fragrance.

Willow shoved her way into my bleak isolation and splashed it with vibrant color. She was here for less than a full day but the impact she had on me will be unforgettable. Now she's gone and I'm alone once again. I should be glad since this was what I wanted. Instead, I feel like my lifeless heart has been jammed in a meat grinder?

If I wanted to be real honest, slivers of hope had started forming in my dejected soul.Even though I didn't let my impassive mask slip and show her how she was affecting me, I thought she might stay.

Why the fuck would she?

I'd been nothing but an asshole from the moment she arrived at my door.

What the fuck am I doing? I can't handle being obsessed with her. I don't need to be more crippled than I already am. I drop the offending scraps of tainted material and move toward to kitchen. Getting blackout wasted sounds like the best way to deal with this shit.

I realize my mistake when the images start seeping into my peripheral. I let my guard down by agonizing over Willow and now I'm going to be punished. I chug the liquor directly from the bottle to speed the process up but I know it's too late.

The visions that flash before my eyes are appalling and cause goosebumps to form on my flesh.

Severed limbs.

Dead eyes.

Choking breath.

Blood pouring out of broken men.

The most horrific are from the few seconds of clarity I had right after the explosion hit. My brothers' faces morphing from shock to excruciating pain. Watching their forms thrown from the vehicle without seeing where they land. The smell of their burning flesh. This is my fucking truth. I deserve this for letting Willow stay. I wish I could say I regretted it.

I didn't think my life could get worse but I was fucking wrong.

The darkness is clawing at me and the psychotic illusions are threatening to pull me under. I take another long swig of whiskey. My brain is a scramble and I can't fucking focus.

The shadows on the wall morph into haunting hallucinations. I dig the heel of my palms into my eye sockets. I punch my skull until I'm dizzy. I yank on my hair until my scalp burns. I can't fucking ignore this crazy shit.

Nothing is fucking working!

I start pacing around the room, clutching my head to try and stop the madness. A stabbing sensation shoots through my temple. Why is this happening to me all the fucking time? I'm not strong enough to endure this shit for the rest of my miserable life. I know I'm the only one who survived but why am I being constantly punished?

When the noises start, I know I'm doomed. I fall to the floor and curl in on myself. My body is shaking uncontrollably and I don't know if I'll survive this time.

Fuck my life.

eleven

willow

I'm sitting at my parent's kitchen table, drinking a cup of hot tea, and absentmindedly tracing lines along the grain with my fingernail. It's the middle of the night so I should be sleeping, but I couldn't get my jumbled thoughts to quiet down. My pulse is pounding while my legs shift nervously under the covers. My mind has been spinning nonstop since coming face to face with Xander the day before. I can't seem to come to terms with how much he's changed.

As soon as I got in my mom's car earlier, she demanded answers. I filled in all the gaps and recapped everything that occurred while I was at his house. Xander's detached persona. Anxious mannerisms. Panic. His blunt coldness. His extreme behaviors. Mood swings. The condition of his house. All of it.

Well, I did leave out the part where I creeped on him while he was splitting wood. She didn't need to know about that.

Any decent psychologist would be thrilled to have such a fascinating case dropped at their feet but I could only worry about what must have happened to cause these drastic differences from the boy I grew up with. Xander was always on the reserved and quiet side. People often didn't grasp his unique personality and thought he was rude, but his athletic abilities and physical appearance provided him with acceptance regardless. Those connections were always surface level though. They weren't interested in getting to know who he really was. Everyone just wanted the status and good looks. Such garbage.

He had a small, tightly knit group of very close friends. Xander didn't mind spending time alone but I never predicted he would one day become a shut in. He was always devastatingly good looking so he had his pick of girls to date. It broke my heart a little more each time he found interest in one enough to keep her around for a while.

Why didn't I ever admit my feelings for him?

The last time I saw Xander, we were twenty years old and still so darn naive about the world. The military was always his plan. He had enlisted in the service when he was eighteen but managed to stay stateside those first two years. When he found out his unit was headed overseas, Xander saw it as an opportunity and a privilege to fight for our country. In addition to getting the chance to protect our freedom, he thrived on order and structure. He was eager to be part of something bigger than any of us.

I was so proud of him but also very concerned about how the war and combat would impact my friend. I have no clue what he was involved in during his tour, which makes me so freaking sad I could start sobbing all over again. I should have voiced my worry. I should have done more for him.

I'm headed back to his place with my dad tomorrow to get my car plowed out of the snow. I wonder if I will get the chance to speak to Xander again. I was so freaking angry and frustrated when I left but I was too harsh in my judgement. My impulsive attitude caused a more compound fracture between our already broken friendship. I'm ashamed of how I acted and admitting that is the first step to fixing it.

I don't think I can handle leaving things between us how they are now. I love that man so much. Even after all this time and with everything that has happened.

I guess I'll see what tomorrow brings.

———— ◆ ————

THE DRIVE BACK to Xander's cabin is fairly uneventful. I'm lost in my thoughts and keeping quiet even though my dad tries grilling me for information. When he doesn't get the hint and makes another attempt to chat, I decide to give in.

"Why do you think Xander is staying all the way out here?" My dad's question shakes me out of my daze because I've been asking myself the same thing.

I shrug my shoulders in defeat. "I have no idea. I tried talking to him but he wasn't interested in divulging any details. Xander hardly spoke to me. To be honest, my visit with him only made me feel worse," I reveal quietly. I turn my face toward the mirror to hide my oncoming tears.

"Willow," my father murmurs, trying to recapture my attention. "Xander will come around. War changes a person but that doesn't mean we have to accept it. He needs to know we care and want to support him. It could take years but healing will happen for him. I know you want to be part of the help he needs, sweetie."

A few drops leak from my eyes and I let them trail down my face. I don't know what to say but I'm saved from responding since we're approaching Xander's place. I mutter a nearly silent, "Thanks, Dad."

Upon arriving, we work fast to get the job done. My body protests as I push my limits with each heaping load of snow I remove. I don't want to risk Xander overreacting about our presence and cause an explosive scene with my father around. An involuntary shiver rushes through me at the thought of him storming out here in a mad rage. I pick up the pace with that image in mind.

My dad easily cleared the excessive amount of snow out of Xander's long driveway. He helped shovel my car out of the pile of white fluff it was buried in before towing it out of the ruts. He made sure I could leave without a problem and then took off for home. All before noon.

Now I'm standing by my driver's side door, pondering my options and feeling really conflicted. Should I just take off without trying to talk to Xander? Or do I try to make amends?

The decision is made for me when I hear a loud crash from inside the house. It isn't just my relentless curiosity that drags me to the front door. I still have deeply instinctive concern for Xander and the combination makes my choice simple. I could never forgive myself if I just walked away without knowing he is all right.

I soon discover he's definitely not.

I don't get a response when I knock and the knob twists easily, which is my first sign that things are definitely not good. I notice how destroyed the room is with my first glimpse inside, which is really saying something. The place was not in great shape to start. It appears that a disastrous storm swept through and wreaked havoc on the meager furnishings spread about. Everything is flipped over, cast aside, or shattered on the ground.

When I spot Xander, I can't keep the sorrowful gasp concealed. My gosh, he looks even worse than yesterday. He's slumped into the corner by his bed and looks to be passed out. Xander's skin is a sickly shade of white and his cheeks are sunken. His clothes are filthy. It smells disgusting in here. Like vomit. Further inspection of the room presents the source of the vile stench. Puke is dripping down the wall near the bathroom.

I slowly walk deeper into the house, careful to avoid stepping on anything. I don't even know where to direct my gaze. Xander groans and shifts slightly on the floor, reassuring me he's at least breathing. I head in his direction then pause a few feet away. He must have heard me enter and approach because I get a reaction from him quickly.

"What the fuck do you want? You left without a backward fucking glance," he wheezes through cracked lips. His eyes are still closed but Xander rolls his neck so his face is turned away from me. His hands are trembling on his thighs and I wish so badly that I could reach out to steady them.

I'm not sure how to respond in order to avoid a hostile altercation. I don't want to set him off. "Xander, I heard a crash and was worried. You didn't answer when I knocked and the door wasn't locked, which really concerned me. I didn't mean to barge in on your privacy again. You have to understand that I care about you and just want to help," I ease out as calmly as possible.

He whips his head towards me once again and his brilliant blues eyes flash open. They are full of fire and look positively livid. So much for keeping it cordial. "How many times do I have to say it, Willow? I don't need your fucking help. I don't want your pity. I don't know why you keep coming back here but just leave me alone. I don't want anything you have to offer." His voice rumbles with more emotion lashing across his pained face. Xander's lip curls into a snarl as he glares at me.

My hands shoot out in front of me in a placating gesture. "I never meant to disrespect you, Xander. You are my friend, even if we haven't seen each other in years. I will never forget what we've been through together. When you were gone, I thought about you constantly. I missed you, Xander. I would never pity you and I am only trying to offer support. Like we always used to do for each other. Please let me be here for you," I plea while trying to control the threat of tears. I can't seem to stop them from flowing around this man.

I swear I can see his shields lock firmly in place as he prepares for a fight. My words seem to have poured gasoline on the coals and now the flames are blazing. It's so frustrating and does a great job drying my moist eyes. Whatever is about to transpire will not be pretty. I can only hope it is somehow cathartic.

"Fuck you, Willow. *Fuck. You.* Stop pretending that you actually want to be here. You don't know me. I don't want you to. I couldn't care less what you say or what you think of me. Our past is fucking irrelevant. I want you gone. Out of my house and out of my life," he roars. Xander is positively seething but I'm not afraid. I can handle the verbal attack he is about to unleash upon me.

I know Xander is pushing me away to get me to leave. He's in so much pain but won't admit it. Heaven forbid he ever ask for help. That is one consistent thread that ties these two versions of Xander together. It gives me hope that I will discover more similarities between the two versions of my friend. He's self-destructing right before my eyes and I can't stop it. I am watching the havoc first-hand and I know I won't leave him again.

Xander struggles to stand and I make no move to help him. It goes against all of my natural impulses, and takes Herculean effort, but I continue to just stand there. His current weakness fuels the rapidly building rage. His eyes are feral and a growl tears from his throat. I shiver uncontrollably and am ashamed that these animalistic tendencies turn me on.

Keep it together, Willow!

My friend is crumbling before me and obviously suffering. He can shove as hard as he wants. Xander can attempt to scare me with his nasty attitude. He can even try to guilt me but I won't budge. In this moment, while I'm staring at this stranger, I am hit with an epiphany.

No matter what, I won't leave him again.

I keep holding strong. "Stop pushing me away, Xander! I'm trying to help and clearly I'm screwing it up. Again. I'm just trying to do the right thing but your dang protective walls are so thick you won't even give me a tiny glimpse. I'm not going anywhere. Can you understand that? You need to find a healthy outlet to let whatever is eating at you escape. Hiding away here won't solve your problems and it's only succeeding in dragging you down deeper. You're stuck in your head with those poisonous thoughts to keep you company."

"Don't try your psycho-babble-bullshit on me, Willow. Been there, done that. You became a therapist, right? Just like your perfect little plan intended? Makes sense why you're trying to stick around. I'm not a new patient for you to fuck with. I deserve to suffer in silence. They all died and I'm alive. Living and breathing. I'm not interested in getting better. You can't fix me." Xander gets closer to me as he continues ranting.

"STOP!" I yell. "I am so frigging sick of talking in circles. I am not trying to analyze you, Xander. For goodness sake. You are important to me and obviously not doing well. It doesn't take someone with a mental health degree to figure that out. Get off your entitled high horse and knock it off. You can't scare me away." My breathing is heavy and I feel like I'm panting. This guy gets me so worked up. I can't stop my slight perusal of his amped up frame.

Xander is glowering at me but takes another step closer. Even though his house reeks and I'm pretty sure he recently spewed all over the wall, Xander has a masculine aura surrounding him that turns me on. He is huge everywhere, which makes me feel so petite and feminine. I can imagine being swallowed up by his bulky body.

What a delicious thought.

Geesh, I am really one to dish out advice when I'm perving on this tormented man.

My ridiculously good looking, *especially* when angry, best friend of a man. With his rugged and disheveled hair that badly needs a trim. Whose hands are so big he could easily palm the entire expanse of my butt. With his bulging muscles that suggest he could effortlessly toss me around. His shoulders are so wide that his shirt is close to tearing at the seams. His grizzly beard only adds to his appeal. I imagine all that coarse hair rasping against my soft skin and leaving evidence of his manly presence.

My extremely sexy, purely platonic pal has an enormous erection tenting his sweatpants.

Wow.

I'm so glad I'm not the only one affected. We take turns devouring each other and I'm not sure how much more I can take.

I need him to act on it. I continue goading him to make sure he's too far gone to stop.

"Use me. You've completely shut yourself off from everything but I'm standing right here. You need to get the anger out, Xander. Let me have it. Don't keep it locked away anymore. It's been trapped too long. You need someone to fire it at? Use me!" My breasts rise with my accelerated breathing. I'm not above begging at this point.

"You better be fucking careful with what you're offering, Willow. I'm not the nice guy I used to be. I will destroy your light and drag you right down with me." Xander is restlessly clenching his hands as he stalks closer. He bites down on his bottom lip as his blue orbs hungrily feast on my chest. Unashamed.

"Good." That's the only response I provide. I curl my lip up in what I hope is an alluring smirk.

That is all the invitation Xander needs. He closes the remaining distance between us with a snarl.

twelve

xander

My eyes ravage Willow's succulent curves and she makes me feel fucking famished. After I get a taste, I'll only crave more. I know I'm headed for further demise by taking what she's offering but I can't seem to give a shit. Sinking deep inside of her and burying myself to the hilt is the only way to satisfy this deprivation.

I have Willow slammed up against the wall as soon as she gives me the green light. She has no fucking clue what she's gotten herself into. I'm furious about all the bullshit she spat my way and her body is about to pay.

"You're in so much fucking trouble. You should have left when you had the chance, Willow," I growl close to her ear. She trembles in my arms. I'm not sure if it's anticipation or fear. Maybe both.

My mouth attacks her neck in a series of vicious bites. I know

I'm being too rough but her breathy moans keep encouraging me. Willow stretches farther to give me better access and I eagerly take advantage. I grab her toned thighs to lift her higher up, closer to where I need her. Willow instantly responds by wrapping her long legs tightly around my waist.

When she starts to grind her hips into me, I lose my fucking mind. This girl has always played the leading role in my fantasies but nothing I ever conjured up does justice to the real deal. Willow is thrashing her head and digging her nails into the wall. She's arching her back so her generous tits smash into my chest. I need to feast on that pillowy flesh.

I grip the hem of her shirt and rip it right down the middle. My barbaric behavior only excites Willow more. I can't understand the unintelligible nonsense spilling from her lips but my attention isn't focused on her mouth.

Her skin is so fucking soft against my rough palms. She's flawless and perfect. I can't wait to make her dirty. My fingers roam up her ribs to squeeze her tempting breasts together. I get the desired effect and it is mouthwatering.

I hike Willow up higher along the wall with a tight grip on her hip and continue grinding my hard into her soft. I bury my nose into the valley between her juicy tits. I get high off her intoxicating scent. A drawn out groan crawls up my throat as I drag my tongue along her. I sink my teeth in and suck hard. She tastes so fucking fantastic. Willow is going wild against me as I worship her body.

"Can I touch you? *Please?*" Her whispered request is a balm to my erratic mind. The fact she even has to ask pisses me off again.

I'm such an asshole.

"Yes. *Fuck yes.* Put your hands on me, Willow. Touch me all you fucking want," I grunt before licking down her jaw. I want my scent covering every inch of her. I return my attention to her chest while my hands grip her ass cheeks in a punishing hold.

When her delicate hands make contact with my shoulders, the anger evaporates. I feel indescribable pleasure descend over me. Even through my shirt, I feel the impact of her touch settle deep within me. I get an overwhelming urge to connect with her in every way possible.

My cock is ready to burst and we're just getting started. I haul her impossibly closer. I dig the solid steel in my pants into the most sensitive part of her. I want *more*.

"Willow, I need to fuck you," I groan between panting gulps. I'm grinding her against me rough and fast. I could easily come from this alone. My grip on her leg and ass is so firm I know I'll leave bruises. With that thought, I suck in a mouthful of skin from her shoulder. I pull and bite hard enough to ensure I'll mark her there as well.

"Yes, yes, please. Do it, Xander. Please!" Willow's shameless begging has me taking immediate action. She sounds delirious and that drives me fucking insane. I can't wait any longer. I need to bury myself deep.

Willow is still wearing too many fucking clothes. I grip the material between her legs and rip until fabric tears away. I shove my pants down just enough for my cock to jut out. I wrap my fist around my rigid shaft and impatiently hover at Willow's entrance.

I invade her wet core in a forceful thrust. Willow's head bangs against the wall with the powerful momentum behind my vigorous movements.

I'm going to *explode*.

"FUCK!" I yell while Willow's mouth gapes open in a silent scream.

I squeeze my eyes shut and grit my teeth. I can't fucking come with the first stroke. Thoughts of Willow getting off from my cock swirl through my mind. I might be an asshole but I've never been selfish while fucking. She's making it really tough with her pussy squeezing my dick in a chokehold. I can confidently say I've never felt anything this fucking amazing before. I let the truth loose.

"Shit, Willow! Your pussy is SO. FUCKING. GOOD!" I punctuate each word with a shallow glide in her silky heat. "I'm going to fucking ruin you!" My brain is mush. I don't even know what type of craziness I'm spewing. All I know is I'm finally deep inside the only girl I ever really wanted.

We aren't having sex. It's definitely not making love. This is angry fucking. With every brutal thrust into her body, the anguish pours out of me and my mind focuses on the pleasure. I am like a man possessed and being forced to take this woman. There is absolutely nothing that could stop this primal act.

Willow's hands start wandering and the sensation of her seductive touch further heightens my arousal. Her fingers glide up my neck and into my hair. She rakes her nails against my scalp before pulling on the roots. I falter and almost lose my hold on her.

Then Willow leans in and gently kisses my chest.

I'm a fucking goner.

She just destroyed me with that move.

Now I am fucking claiming her and Willow gladly signs over her rights.

I grip her hips and slam her down onto me even harder. Skin is slapping loudly and echoing throughout the room. I would be concerned I was hurting Willow but her intoxicating noises prove she is in pure ecstasy. I lock my teeth onto her earlobe and growl as the hunger threatens to take over. I want to own this woman. Entirely.

I'm conquering her body, dominating her mind, and commanding her soul. Willow is fucking *mine*.

I bring my hand down to where we are connected to feel her tiny body taking my massive cock. The strong suction makes my balls tighten. I could get off on hearing how soaked she is. My fingers slide through her drenched seam and rub her swollen clit. Willow starts bucking against me and becomes even more frenzied.

I'm relentless as my shaft fiercely pounds into her. My hand is still wedged between us and focused on blowing her mind. Willow begins to shake uncontrollably as I furiously attack her clit.

I resume biting and sucking any exposed flesh she is offering. I can't hold off much longer. I hitch one of her legs higher on my waist to change the angle and that effectively propels Willow over the edge.

"Xander, please, please! Keep going, harder! Yes, yes, YES!" Her screams shove me off the ledge of sanity and I free-fall into her body. I'm thrusting wildly as my come shoots into her desperate pussy. Continuous jets stream out to coat her walls with *me*. My release seems to keep going until finally I can't stay upright any longer. Willow collapses with me on the floor in a pile of limbs and bodily fluids.

Our heavy breathing is the only sound surrounding us. We lay there for countless moments, not in any hurry to move. I'm trying to collect my shattered thoughts over what the fuck just happened.

My arms are wrapped protectively around Willow. She's still stroking through my hair, which is so fucking soothing I could almost fall asleep. Her fingers are so delicate and careful in their movements. Like she's comforting me. Regret pools in my stomach as shame slams into me.

Holy shit.

I just fucked Willow, and I do mean *fucked*. I can feel my seed seeping out of her onto my leg. There was nothing nice about what just happened between us.

The urge to escape overwhelms me. I can't handle the look of disgust that I'm sure is marring her beautiful face. There is no doubt Willow is offended by that depraved act I just forced upon her. The panic causes my heart to take off at an alarming pace.

Sheer terror over what happens next has the darkness blurring my vision.

I'm so disgusting.

With that thought as motivation, I untangle from her body and run for the door.

thirteen

willow

One moment I'm totally blissed out, wrapped in Xander's arms. The next I'm being dumped on the freezing floor as he flees. Again.

What the heck?!

That jerk took off almost as soon as he came inside of me.

Without a condom!

He's darn lucky I'm on birth control. Xander better not try pushing me away after what we just shared. I've never experienced anything even close to that, whatever *that* even was. I thought we actually made progress by engaging in such an intense act. There is no way he can actually believe I will let him pull this disappearing crap. Nope, not happening. We are going to freaking talk about this one way or another.

My shirt is destroyed so I grab a discarded bedsheet and wrap it tightly around my body. I am so fuming mad as I storm off after Xander that my face feels lit with flames. My blood turns to burning lava as I prepare for a battle. When I yank open the door, I am fully prepared to release all of my aggravation on him but the words die in my throat.

Xander is anxiously pacing barefoot in the deep snow, making a clear path with each step. He's yanking hard on his hair and muttering under his breath. I'm not sure if he's aware of my presence. Xander appears consumed by his thoughts and lost to anything else. I fear that whatever is holding him captive is beginning to take control. Raw pain is openly exposed on his face as he clenches his eyes shut.

I slowly walk closer to him while calling his name in an attempt to gain his attention. Xander's distressed stride does not falter or slow. I tentatively reach my hand out to grasp his arm, fully aware of the potential repercussions. I'm shocked when his restless movements instantly stop. Xander's concentration is focused on my fingers against his skin. I hope this is still all right and it wasn't just because his guard was down during sex. Maybe it's a good time to ask.

"Is it alright that I'm touching you?" I breathe out, feeling the nerves bubble in my stomach.

Xander lifts his cobalt eyes to look at me and shrugs. "It's different with you somehow. I've had a fucking aversion to people's touch for years but with you, it's the opposite. I don't fucking understand and I can't describe it." His admission seems to flow out of him without permission. I'm totally taken by surprise with what Xander just revealed. My stunned silence seems to have his anxiety creeping back in as his hands begin to tremble.

"Does that freak you out, Willow? I didn't mean to make you more uncomfortable than I already have." His stare is so laser focused that I swear he is looking deep into my soul. I mentally shake off the impact of his words so I can enjoy the openness Xander is offering.

"You have no idea what that means to me, Xander. To be honest, I am a little unsure of what to say. I am still in shock over what happened between us before you stormed out here. To have that type of impact on someone, especially you, is mind boggling. It makes me feel really special and I like that. Probably too much." I bring my free hand to my forehead and try to gather my thoughts.

"What do you mean by that? *Especially you?*" Xander inquires as soon as I stop speaking.

I choke on my tongue as the secret I've held far too long tries to escape.

He doesn't really expect me to lay everything out and admit all of my feelings after our rocky reunion, right?

I go with a safer explanation.

"Well, you know, we were once best friends and you always meant so much to me. To know you might still care about me on some subconscious level really resonates within me, Xander." Our eyes are locked and something monumental seems to pass between us.

He takes a step closer and I shiver from his dominating presence. The memory of what just transpired inside the house has a blush rising to my cheeks. If Xander notices, he doesn't mention it.

"Willow, I've been really shitty ever since you first knocked on my door. I can't control my anger and I have all these screwed up thoughts constantly fucking with my mind. I'm a disaster, which is why I tried so hard to keep you away. There's so much that's happened and the man I used to be is long gone. I didn't want to hurt you but now it's too late. I shouldn't have taken advantage of you like that." He juts his chin toward the door, referring to the crazy escapdes we just had, before continuing.

"Now everything is even more screwed up, which I didn't realize was possible considering how messed up I already am." He finishes with a distraught grunt.

His stance looks so sad and unsettled. The deep frown marring his handsome face breaks me apart. I want to wrap him in a tight hug but I'm not sure if that would actually help.

Xander's distracted gaze bounces between my eyes and lips. The tension between us gains strength and becomes a living force. I lean further into his body to gain warmth, but mostly so I can rub along his naked flesh.

It's then I realize we haven't even kissed. That kind of sets me off but in a weird way it makes me feel naughty. He pounded me into the wall but our mouths never met. That is definitely something to bring up later.

Gosh, this is all so bizarre.

We need to work together to make sense of all this. "You didn't take advantage, Xander. I was a very willing participant and if I recall correctly, it was me that pushed you. I wanted everything you gave me and I loved what we just did. I didn't want gentle or soft. I wanted you to unleash some of that brutal anger you harbor inside. Don't you dare feel guilty. What I'm most concerned about is that we were always just friends and now those lines are very blurred. When I got here today, I wasn't sure if we would ever talk again. Now, I feel like we're in a strange place. I would love to spend time with you, Xander. I don't expect anything other than trying to get to know who you are again. Is that something you would be cool with?" I couldn't keep the hope out of my voice even if I tried.

I kept holding Xander's gaze, which was intently focused on my eyes while I spoke. I have no clue how he'll react to what I just suggested. All I wanted was my friend back.

All right, that's totally bogus.

I will never forget how it felt to have him buried deep inside me. I'd never been stretched so wide as my body acclimated to his generous size. The pinch of pain blended smoothly within the layers of pleasure. I'm getting wet just thinking about his hard thrusts into my soft center. I'm not sure how I will keep my true feelings hidden when I'm in this vulnerable state.

What a disaster!

"I don't know what to say, Willow. I just brutally fucked you in my disgusting house. I'm such a bastard for treating you that way. Once upon a time, you were very special to me and you deserve so much better than what I did. You need so much more than the broken man I've become. I don't even know how to be around people anymore. I'm not even sure I can mentally handle having you around. Saying it aloud makes me feel so fucking insane." Xander breathed out a heavy sigh and scrubbed his palm against his rugged beard. His ocean eyes reflected sorrow within their depths.

"I want you to have some decent memories of me and I fear if you spend more time here, I will tarnish even the best moments we shared. I know it is engrained in you to help others and try to fix their problems. I'm sure you're an excellent therapist. I think you should just leave and forget about me." He drops his eye contact with that last statement and it breaks my heart to see him so forlorn.

His angry mask slips away and now I'm witnessing the misery trapped within. I'm not sure how it will work quite yet but I need to stick around to try rebuilding our bond.

I squeeze his arm to get his attention back. "Xander, we just keep going in circles. We've come to an impasse and I refuse to walk away with so much still left unsaid. Let me at least help you clean up inside. You can't convince me you'd rather manage that mayhem alone. Once we're done, we can talk more about . . . whatever is going on. Sound fair?" I need him to agree. To let me begin helping him, even with this small task.

I can already tell he is going to argue with me before he even starts. "Willow, listen . . ." I cut him off before he can say more. I have to hold back the urge to stamp my foot.

"No. I'm going to help you because you're my friend. Not a client or a patient. I will never, *ever* see you that way. I promise. Please don't let your toxic thoughts trick your mind into believing otherwise. Please let me be here for you. At least just for a little bit."

I grab his shaking hand with my free one in an attempt to settle him. Xander slams his lids closed and gives his head a slight shake. When he reopens his eyes, they are clear and focused.

"You have no fucking clue what you're walking into, Willow. I'm a blasted hurricane set to destroy anything in my path. Why would you want to stay?" He's so hesitant and resistant but I know he needs me here. I push a little harder.

"Please, Xander. You think so poorly of yourself but I know you. Deep down you're still the boy I used to know. We just have to find him. Let me help you." I squeeze his palm for emphasis.

Even though Xander is apprehensive, I am looking forward to what lies ahead.

His furrowed brow and gritted teeth reveal he's wavering. "I'm having a difficult time saying no, even though I can predict the fucking destruction. If you really want to hang around longer, I won't deny you. I've already warned you plenty of times." Xander rubs his fingers across his drooping eyes before coming to a decision.

"Lead the way," he tells me while sweeping his arm in the direction of the open door.

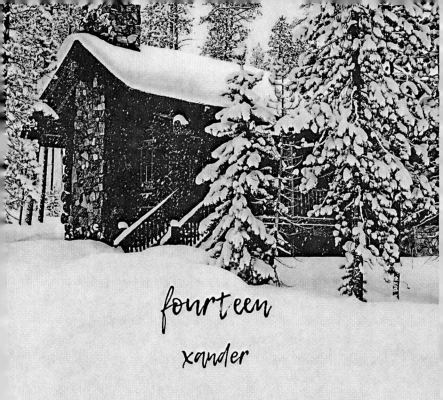

fourteen

xander

What the fuck is happening?

That incessant question keeps badgering me and I don't have a fucking clue how to answer. All I know is Willow is in my house, cleaning up my mess, and seems really pleased about it.

When we first came back in, Willow moved about my house like she's lived here for years. She knows where everything goes, without having to ask, as she flits around the small rooms. Willow made herself comfortable with ease and fits right into my space.

She had another outfit in her car so she changed out of her ruined clothes. She looks all put back together and orderly. I don't like it. I preferred the disheveled, freshly fucked looked so I want to shred every stitch covering her.

Since Willow touched me earlier, the darkness has left me alone and the panic has stayed away. Now I'm fucked up for a totally different reason and she's currently smiling at me from the kitchen. I completely isolated myself out here for damn good reasons but I am having a tough time thinking of them with her beaming at me.

Willow has my full attention but maybe that isn't such a bad thing. I've only had myself to rely on lately and had been getting along in my own way. I'd been adamant that I didn't need help or support from anyone but the thought of her leaving makes my gut clench. I should be pissed as shit that I am already affected by her again. On some level I am angry that I can't seem to turn her away, but the calming sensation she gives me outweighs the fury.

My mind is clogged with the overwhelming confusion I'm dealing with. After having sex with Willow, I freaked the fuck out. My younger self would be ashamed of how I treated her. I used to obsess over how perfect it would be when we finally slept together. I was such a fucking dreamer. Look at how great all that fantasizing turned out.

Fucking terrible.

I don't care what Willow says, there's no way what I did to her was what she really wanted. I should have been gentle and sweet. I could have taken more time to prepare her. There was always so much I wanted to do but I'm not that type of man anymore. All I'm good for is rough, dirty, and harsh. Willow deserves much better than any pathetic shit I can provide.

The fact we were friends before makes this situation even more despicable. She is a romance junkie and loves to be spoiled, which I've known since we were kids. I can't give her what she's always dreamed up for her happily ever after. Not even fucking close. Willow believes we can rebuild our bond but I've never screwed one of my pals before. I won't be able to remove those sexy as fuck memories we just created. Even if we go back to just being friends.

Considering going back to strictly platonic with Willow has

me grinding my teeth. A moment ago I didn't think I could stand having her in my space and now I want to fuck her again? I need to get a fucking grip.

Willow starts humming and it brings me back to my current surroundings. Why is she so happy cleaning my house? I can't concentrate for shit but she appears to be perfectly content and pleased beyond belief. I can't bite my tongue any longer.

"Willow?" I begin the conversation by stealing her focus. Once she turns to face me, I dive right in. "What the fuck is happening?" I decide to just ask the question that has been circling my mind for the last thirty minutes.

She startles slightly from my blunt approach but responds smoothly as if she was prepared for it. "I thought we made it pretty clear before coming back in here. I'm helping tidy up the wreck you created. Is that still alright?" Her question seems innocent enough but I remember how sharp she is. There is always a deeper meaning hiding beneath the surface with her.

"You know I wasn't that willing to let you stay at first but yes, I'm fine with it. What I meant was what is happening between us? What is going on? You are sweeping around the room like all is well while I sit here extremely fucking irritated. I'm not trying to be an asshole but I can't take the confusion piled on top of all the other shit I'm already dealing with." The aggravation and frustration are starting to take over. I can't allow her to watch me crash into the abyss.

I take a deep breath before continuing. "*Fuck*. I'm sorry, Willow. I'm not used to having conversations anymore. I'm totally out of my element and I don't fucking like it."

She keeps quietly assessing me with her emerald gaze, which unnerves me further. My sanity slips farther away and the edges of my vision start to blur.

Shit, shit shit . . .

I jerk slightly when I feel her soft hand cover my tightened fist before slipping around my wrist. The sweet serenity creeps in and chases the darkness away. Willow's effect on me still freaks me out, and I have no idea how to explain it, but I am relieved the panic has subsided.

For now.

The concern etched on her features is genuine and I consider that Willow might still care about me. I don't know how or understand why but maybe I can rely on her slightly. I wouldn't have to be totally detached anymore. I could try spending time with her and attempt getting to know each other again.

The fear of being vulnerable is at the forefront of my mind as I contemplate my options. The choices seem extremely limited as I stare at the beautiful woman in front of me. If she wants to be present in my fucked up life, I can't stop her and I don't want to either.

The silence between us has stretched on far too long to be comfortable but it doesn't seem to bother Willow. I want to know what she's thinking but am too afraid to ask. I get trapped in the gold flecks accenting her green irises and lose my train of thought. For a stupid moment, I feel like the horny teenager that used to gobble up any scrap of attention Willow would toss my way. I groan loudly at the nonstop chaos in my mind.

I need some space. I can't continue with this ludicrous train of thought. As I begin to mentally and physically distance myself from Willow, she breaks our muted standoff.

"There is so much going on up there. I can almost see the gears turning. Can't we just be still for a little while?" She taps my temple while speaking.

I try to explain some of my madness. "Earlier you said we were talking in circles but that's what I always feel like. I can't seem to make sense of anything, which bothers the shit out of me. Trying to figure out what you're thinking is stretching me even further. I'm going for a walk, alright? Just to quiet some of the turmoil." My voice is low as I back farther away from her. When her arm is fully extended and about to drop due to the distance between us, Willow stops me.

"Xander, wait. Why don't you ask me what you're wondering?" She pulls me back toward her and I'm unsure how to react.

I decide to swallow my bullshit and go for it.

"What were you thinking about, Willow? What is causing that questioning look to cover your face?" My eyes sweep over her as I anxiously await her response.

Why is her answer so damn important? I don't know why I care so fucking much but I can't seem to control my impulses where Willow is concerned.

She leans into my personal space so she can whisper close to my ear, "I want you to kiss me."

fifteen

willow

Boldness thrums through me as those simple words leave my lips. I have no clue where I got the courage to let my desires surface but I love it. Xander isn't the only one being impacted by our connection. He makes me want to be risky, brave, and strong. The blistering heat behind his stare proves his attraction and I'm done waiting. I'm ready to take on anything.

I've let go of my insecurities and now it's his turn. Xander has to be in control of what happens next. I need to know he wants it too. I've discovered Xander's way of coping is a quick getaway but I won't let him go without a fight. Based on his tense posture and the restless shuffling of his feet, I know Xander wants to dodge this confrontation. His nerves are tangible with each fidget and tremble of his arms.

We have so much to talk about but those conversations need to be a team effort. Xander is clearly not ready. Fooling around will further confuse our situation but it seems like the easiest way to engage with him at this point. I'm not going to complain.

My irresponsible behavior is dangerous for my delicate heart but self-preservation has always been a weakness of mine. I won't deny the physical pull my body has to Xander and the compulsion to have his plump lips covering mine. I cannot stay away from this man, no matter what it costs me. It seems borderline obsessive, this driving need I have, but all I want is to bring him back from the darkness. If all this leads to helping Xander, it will be worth anything I have to give. My love for this man is overpowering.

When I step back to gauge his reaction, I shiver at the expression on his face. His chiseled jaw is taut, his nostrils flare with his uneasy breathing, but it's his eyes that give away the depth of his feelings. The vivid blue is smoldering and setting fire to my core.

Without a word, Xander slowly shifts closer to me. His glance bounces around my features but mainly focuses on my slight pout. The anticipation of watching him move toward me inch by inch has my impatience skyrocketing. I want to close the distance hovering between us badly, but I wait.

He makes me feel so beautiful in his unique way. The little signals, like the flare of his nostrils and the barely-there tint to his cheeks, cause my heart to flutter. Xander's teeth grind together as his fists clench, as though he has to force himself to hold back. The very obvious bulge at his groin has my insides practically melting.

Xander's beard scratches my cheek as he brushes against me. I can tell he is wound tight by the bunch of his corded muscle where I'm still gripping his arm. My lids flutter closed when his mouth lightly dusts the edge of my lips. I remain completely still while he continues giving me soft pecks before covering my mouth completely with his.

Within those first few moments, our lips are simply pressed together but my mind is already fuzzy with arousal. This gentle touch from him is incredible. Xander starts gliding his mouth over mine, as if testing our connection. Then he angles his head a smidge before sucking on my bottom lip. My stomach twists in stunned somersaults as the overwhelming sensations flood my system all at once.

A moan rumbles in my throat and the sound seems to snap the ties holding Xander back. His hand spears into my hair and pulls my mouth impossibly closer. His tongue slides along the seam of my lips before I eagerly open my mouth. There is a battle of power as we attack each other and get wrapped up in a tornado of lust. The silky push and the sucking pull are driving me wild. I had no idea kissing could feel so freaking amazing.

My arms are wound around Xander's huge shoulders so I'm able to feel the tension seep out of his body. Even though he seems more relaxed, his solid form is still rock-hard beneath my wandering hands. *Everywhere.* The evidence of his arousal is digging into my pelvis and it matches my restless enthusiasm. I tremble at the reminder of what Xander has hidden in those pants as my panties grow damper, almost embarrassingly wet at this point. I'm getting even more turned on knowing I have such an obvious effect on him.

His other hand runs along the bottom of my shirt before slowly easing underneath the fabric. His calloused fingertips rasp at the sensitive skin on my torso. I arch into him simply because his touch is teasing and makes my body hum with electricity. Even though Xander is showing me a softer side, there's still a rough edge to his movements that ratchets up my excitement even more.

Xander's palm rubs back and forth a few times before wrapping around my hip. Then his digits are reaching into the back of my leggings to grip my butt. He yanks my body into his and grinds our hips together. This seems so familiar but his approach is more intentional than last time. It's as though he is mapping my flesh and wants it all stamped as his. As if I could forget his presence.

His groan vibrates in his chest and slides over me like a warm caress.

He loves this.

It's obvious in every move he makes and sound he emits. Xander is worshiping me with this kiss and completely obliterating any hesitations I might have had in the back of my mind. He's devouring me slowly and taking his time to explore. The control he's displaying by holding back his overwhelming power shows how much he cares for me. He isn't pressuring me to go faster or forcing his body deeper into mine.

I feel like time has been suspended. With every slide of his tongue, I'm sucked deeper into the fog. I am totally lost in this kiss and nothing else registers.

Seriously, why don't adults make out more often?

Xander growls while sucking my lip between his teeth. He gives my butt a light slap before withdrawing his hand from my pants. When we break apart, I take a deep inhale before opening my eyes. I'm embarrassingly aroused and I'm sure the flush covering my face is a dead giveaway. Xander is staring at me with a look so sincere it makes my breath hitch. I manage to clear my throat and let the words tumble out.

"So, can I stay?" I ask in a barely there whisper, afraid of rejection for my fragile heart.

"Yes."

Just yes, but that's all I needed.

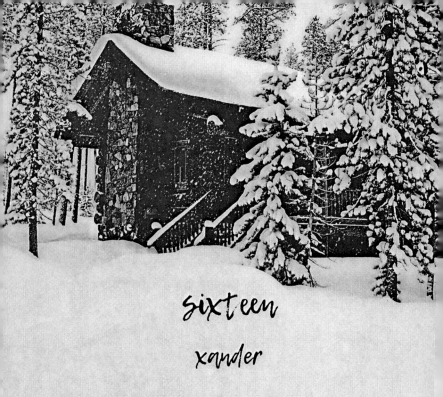

sixteen

xander

I'm still wound up from that fucking kiss and I don't know what to do with myself. I'm restless, anxious, and totally on edge. I agreed to let Willow stay but I have no idea what that means. Did she mean for a few hours? A day? A week?

All I need are more uncertainties to stress about.

After exchanging a few tense words after I agreed to let her stay, Willow went back to cleaning. She never was good at sitting still and that obviously hasn't changed. I suppose I'm not either since I feel like jumping out of my fucking skin. I'll probably wear through the floorboards with all my neurotic pacing.

I never used to be an overly emotional guy. I told it how it was and didn't beat around the bush. I expected the same in return. I was told my brutal honesty insulted people but I didn't understand the purpose of spewing a bunch of bullshit to spare someone's feelings. The only thing I ever held back was love for

Willow, which fucked up my life real great. I should have stuck to my typical rules and confessed years ago, to hell with any consequences.

Apparently I don't have a social filter but it never bothered the gorgeous girl in front of me. When Willow told me what she'd been thinking, I figured I hadn't offended her as badly as I originally assumed. I had another opportunity to prove I wasn't a complete savage. This time I wouldn't fucking push it. She asked for a kiss and that's all she was getting. I didn't want to give her further ammunition against me if shit went sour. Considering it further, those good intentions should be tossed out the boarded up window.

As soon as our mouths collided, it was a true test to my restraint. The temptation to fuck her again was extremely powerful but I managed to keep my shit in check. Allowing myself to grope her ass definitely didn't hurt. I can still taste her cherry gloss on my lips and it makes me desperate for more.

What a fucking kiss.

Damn.

My cock is still rock hard and replaying our kiss isn't helping.

Taking a walk sounds like a great plan since I didn't get the chance earlier. The freezing weather and expansive landscape were sure to cool off my raging hormones. I move closer to the door but abruptly stop before opening it because my legs lock in place. Leaving Willow seems like an impossible task that I'm not sure I want to accomplish. I groan loudly at the pussy whipped habits that are already taking over because her presence isn't a fucking guarantee.

"Did you say something, Xander?" Willow asks over her shoulder from where she's folding scattered clothing near my bed.

Just great.

She's probably witnessing the stupid conflict I'm having with myself.

I try to keep the discomfort out of my voice. "I was thinking of taking a walk but maybe I should stay to finish cleaning."

I'm such an idiot.

Willow is laughing as she turns to face me. "That's a good one. I would gladly accept your help but I think I'm almost done. Maybe we could go outside together in a bit?"

The thought of her tagging along feeds the crazy codependency rapidly forming. I'm glad she suggested it because it saves my pansy ass from having to admit stuff I'm not ready to. It's too early for me to assume that Willow doesn't want to be away from me either. The trauma and demons force me to believe she could never want to stay with me but I'm starting to build strength against them.

"All right. This isn't easy for me but I'm doing my best not to freak out. I smell like shit so maybe I should rinse off instead." I cross my arms over my chest in a defensive move against the sudden onslaught of anxiety. I wait a moment for Willow's response since she always has one.

When the silence continues, I take a closer look at her since my mind is fucking spinning and assuming the worst. Willow is rarely quiet, unless she is up to something, so I'm immediately suspicious. As a blush appears on her cheeks, Willow ducks her chin in order to hide from me. Her succulent bottom lip is trapped between her teeth and her hips shift slightly. I can't help but wonder if she's imagining me in the shower.

Even a fucked up guy can hope.

I walk into the bathroom, shut the door behind me, and exhale a shaky breath. When I catch sight of the broken mirror, any lingering lust vanishes and dread slams into my gut. I can't stand the sight of my reflection so the glass was shattered when I first moved in. I have no interest in viewing the monster I've become, the disturbing man that will now stare back at me. My vision starts to grow hazy as I imagine what made me this way.

Even though my clothes are masking the damage, I know what's lurking beneath. The scars covering my body seem to burn with recognition and remind me of the battle I lost. Not bothering to delay the inevitable, I pull the shirt over my head and yank the sweatpants down my hips. I scour the ruin marring the skin of my torso, chest, arms, and shoulders. My back is camouflaged in old wounds but thankfully I can't fixate on them.

I stand completely still as the memories swarm my mind. Tears burn my eyes as I picture my fallen brothers. All of them deteriorating to dust before me and I'm again helpless to stop the destruction. My body threatens to buckle and collapse with the weight of it all.

I examine the thick jagged line that starts at my left pec and grotesquely zigzags until it ends near my right ribs. Even after a year, the surrounding flesh looks irritated and infected. I still wonder how I survived considering how nasty that fucking gash appears.

The canvas of wreckage matches the tragic catastrophe I'm harboring inside. I'll never escape the fucking desert and the ghosts lingering within the shadows. The gurgling screams blend with disfigured faces will forever haunt me. My legs finally give out and I crash down to my knees.

I'll never escape.

I'm so far gone that I don't hear the door open behind me. The telltale gasp alerts me that Willow is getting her first glimpse of what I've become. I don't even attempt to cover my exposed shame. I bow my head and wait for her inevitable disgust to be verbalized. How could she not be filled with loathing upon witnessing this scene? The revulsion bubbles in my gut as I prepare for her to leave, just like I knew she would.

Fuck.

seventeen

willow

A loud bang steals my attention from the pile of clothes in front of me. My head snaps toward the location of the sound and I'm instantly on alert. Even though I can't see him, I know something alarming just happened in there. The water isn't running and it's eerily quiet as I near the bathroom.

I'm definitely noticing a trend since I've been here. I tend to waltz into these startling situations, unsuspecting of the potential risks. This is reminiscent of when I found Xander panicking after we had sex. What will I stumble upon this time? I hear another disturbing clatter loudly echo through the small space, which propels me forward.

Formalities and etiquette flew out the window when I first arrived so I don't knock on the door before opening it. I edge into the bathroom totally unprepared for the sight before me. Again. The startled gasp leaps from my throats before I even realize it.

Xander is kneeling on the floor in a defeated position and tenses further from my sound. His big body is hunched over and curled in a distinctively protective manner. My frantic gaze doesn't settle on his position because I'm too preoccupied scanning for injuries.

My eyes barely register the scars littering most of Xander's upper body because something much more fascinating has caught my attention. I silently study the intricate tattoo that covers a huge portion of his right side. The dark lines start at his forearm before growing up his upper arm and wrapping around his bicep. From there it branches out to flow onto his pec and extends to his shoulder. The ink reaches around his back to complete the enormous work of art.

It's absolutely mesmerizing and I am stunned by the creative beauty. I inch forward to get a closer look to determine what the design is. I'm a bit puzzled by my findings because I can't comprehend the hidden meaning. The tattoo definitely resembles an exotic tree.

It's so freaking stunning!

Another gasp slips out without warning. "Oh my gosh, Xander!" I don't know what else to say. I'm a little stunned. That's for sure. My curiosity sprouts like an annoying pest that I can't get rid of as I continue investigating his arm.

Why didn't I see this before?

What does this tree mean to him?

After hearing my exclamation, Xander snaps out of his silent stupor to lash out. "I know I'm a fucking freak. The fucked up disaster outside matches the messed up mayhem in my mind. When are you going to believe me that you should just leave?" His tone is feral and I'm suddenly heavy with disappointment that he's reverted back to this defense mechanism.

At first I don't understand why he's so angry. I'm sure he doesn't appreciate me drooling all over him. It takes monumental effort to look away from the intricate tattoo but then I scan over the collection of gashes, scars, and wounds that decorate the rest of Xander's skin. It looks like a horrible scrapbook of memories he's desperate to forget.

My mind is a blank slate as I scramble for what to say. I need to do something but my body remains locked in place. Xander hangs his head before his shoulders slump forward further. He appears to be in an extremely vulnerable state and I don't want to make it worse. I am so freaking confused. Maybe it would be better for me to give him space. Selfishly, I don't think I can. Just thinking of leaving him like this makes my chest ache. I need to reach him before he gets pulled farther into this madness.

"Let me see you, Xander," I whisper. *"Please."*

He doesn't respond so I try to be patient while surveying my options. His eyes are squeezed shut and his fists quiver as he fights the battle against his mind. I need him to understand that I don't see the damage when my gaze feasts on his glorious form. He could never be a monster to me, no matter what horrible poison fills his head.

I shuffle forward a few feet to lean against the vanity. Xander has his face averted and clearly doesn't want to chat. He's disappeared into his mind and is allowing his crippling thoughts to take over.

My limited interactions with Xander have been strained but have provided some explanation into these erratic shifts in his character. I've witnessed similar behavior from patients with severe trauma. I hate comparing Xander to cases I've worked with but in these instances, my experience has proven useful. It's clear that all he can see right now are the flaws. He's trained himself to believe that he's ruined and worthless.

Xander seems to forget how well I know him and that I'm aware of who he is, buried deep within. That's what I truly care about. It's Xander's beautiful heart that I want. The scars are just superficial. What truly defines him has nothing to do with the markings on his flesh. Other than the newly discovered ink . . .

I desperately want to get a closer look at his tattoo.

I hesitantly reach out to trace the delicate details of the tree but stop before my fingers touch his skin. It's absolutely magnificent. The winding roots merge into a swirling trunk with endless branches and eccentric twigs. Each line is perfectly placed to create the extraordinary piece. I can't believe he didn't tell me about this sooner. Alright, that's laughable but honestly, I can't imagine him permanently getting this symbol etched into his arm for no reason. The Xander I always knew wouldn't impulsively choose some random item. There has to be a story that goes along with it.

When did he get this done?

I'm so effing curious about this ink embedded into him but clearly Xander is not in the mood to explain. I'll add it to the growing list of topics to readdress at a more appropriate time. My head spins as I attempt to gather my scattered ideas.

Xander's body is still locked up as he remains closed off. He's full of so much hate and fury. He's bottled it up so tight that I'm worried he's about to implode. His entire form begins to tremble and shake as he cowers on the bathroom floor. Xander is trapped in such a horrible place and can't find an escape route. I don't know how much longer I can watch this without intervening, forget the consequences.

Ever since I found out Xander was back, I've been desperate for a cozy hug. The type that steals your breath and leaves you tingling with warmth. It used to be our thing and I miss it terribly. I've wanted to jump into his arms and spin around like a cheesy romantic comedy.

Obviously, I've realized that would be about as well received as an ice bath, so I've held off. There isn't anything for me to fear from this man, not anymore. Based on recent observations,

Xander has a specialty in attacking himself and it's slowly breaking my heart.

I'm not waiting another minute.

I descend on his broken form and tightly wrap my arms around him. Overwhelming warmth engulfs me as I pull Xander close to me. I've craved this simple affection, though I'd rather have it happen on better terms, I'll take what I can get.

At first Xander stiffens and my gut clenches in feat that he will reject me. I'm sure it isn't easy for him to accept my touch in this dark moment. But the change is drastic and sudden. His glacial exterior cracks open and all the pain seems to purge out rapidly.

Gut wrenching sobs echo off the tiled floor. Xander's body is heaving with his ragged cries and I'm astonished by the flood of crushing emotion before me. The broken noises ripping from his throat break my heart but his is exactly what he needs to release his demons. The tears soaking into my shoulder are evidence of the pain he's held onto for too long.

When I imagine what could cause such a significant reaction, my mind instantly goes to horrible places I've heard from my job. I'm only a bystander to this onslaught of agony but it cuts me deep regardless. My chest aches with empathy for what he's currently going through but I'm relieved he's letting it out. The wounded layers seem to shed away with each quiver of his skin.

I whisper soothing words close to Xander's ear while rubbing his back. Maybe they aren't registering but I want him to know I will always support him. No matter what, I'll be here to love him. I continue softly stroking his skin while he is fisting the material of my shirt. I grip him tighter and hold with all my might. I need to be his solid ground while he's slipping off the edge.

I lose track of time as Xander keeps releasing his anguish with convulsing tremors. I can only hope he's finding some relief in this and it's helping him heal. Even though my legs are cramping and my arms are strained, I don't move or complain. I can handle the temporary discomfort if it means Xander is finding some semblance of peace.

Eventually his sounds of sorrow taper off but he doesn't release me. His hands smooth over my sides and ease around my lower back. Xander shifts slightly, which allows me to adjust my sore limbs. I never lose contact with his skin and once we're settled again, I dig my fingers into his muscles. He turns his head so his lips are nearly touching my neck.

"Thank you, Willow." His raspy voice cracks. He clears his throat before speaking again. "I'm really overwhelmed right now. That was so fucked up I should be ashamed. My head is clear for a change. That's thanks to you."

He places a gentle kiss against my sensitive skin and I quickly angle my face to hide my own onslaught of grief.

eighteen

xander

As I sit on the freezing floor, cocooned in Willow's arms, my mind is once again bogged down in warped confusion.

What the hell was that?

With Willow here, I'm constantly questioning myself and obsessing over stupid bullshit. I know this reality is far better than how I was coping alone but the twisted feelings make it difficult to settle down.

I just bawled my fucking eyes out like an inconsolable child and I couldn't seem to stop. Once I crumbled, the despair and suffering immediately started draining out. I couldn't turn them off. I cried and fucking cried until I felt rubbed raw. I purged all the pain I'd been harboring and I'll admit, relief is beginning to flow inside me. I just don't know what to do now that I openly broke down in front of Willow. She's going to want answers that

I'm not ready to give.

Willow moves a bit, which effectively reminds me of our current predicament. Not that I could ever forget. She's trying to hide her tears for some reason. I have no clue how she could be embarrassed after the show I put on for her. If I was a better man, I would ask and not let her go on pretending she's fine. I could take a turn offering comfort but I'm sure I'll fuck it up.

I suddenly realize that I am naked. Willow is practically straddling me and my body is beginning to take notice. Her sinful curves are pressed up against me and in close proximity to my rapidly hardening dick. I don't need her assuming all I want is sex, especially when she's crying. I've had enough shame for today.

It physically pains me to loosen my hold and put some much needed distance between us. Willow whines in protest, which is like a knife cutting into my heart.

I try to soften the blow as I pull away. "Before this gets more awkward for me, I'm going to take a shower. We can talk when I'm done, all right?" I'm growing more uncomfortable the longer we continue sitting here.

Thankfully Willow takes my not so subtle hint and lifts herself from my lap. I try to cover myself but then realize there's no point. I'm completely exposed but she's already seen it all. My insanity, my scars, and my junk are on full display. The willow tree covering my arm has been hidden from her since she arrived but she clearly saw that too. She didn't comment on the design so maybe she hasn't figured out the meaning. I'll have to fucking tell her soon enough regardless.

Fuck it.

I stand on shaky legs and lean against the wall to turn on the water. My skin itches and I'm feeling so fucking stressed with Willow lingering. My heart pounds as I wonder if she's figured out the truth behind my ink. I look at her over my shoulder and catch her ogling my ass. She freezes and an obvious blush blooms on her cheeks. I can almost feel a smile forming on my lips and that freaks me out even further.

Willow's face turns red with embarrassment and she stutters out an apology before rushing from the room. When the door clicks shut, some of the tension seeps out of me. Then I get the urge to invite her back in just to have her close.

I'm so fucked up.

She's still in the house, idiot.

Jumping in the shower, I race through my usual routine. I'd never admit that I'm anxious when she's out of my sight, but Willow has definitely knocked something loose. As I finish up, I try not to overthink this new level of wacked I've stooped to. I mop up the trickles of water trailing down my body before wrapping the towel around my waist.

As the door is ripped open, my eyes immediately seek out Willow. She's in the kitchen searching through my sorry excuse for a refrigerator. For a moment I'm distracted by her swaying ass as she bends to check the bottom shelf. Then the guilt sets in for not thinking to offer her food sooner. As if I could forget my incompetence.

I leave her be and turn to my bedroom to get dressed. I grab the first clean clothes I find and carelessly throw them on. I casually glance around and notice how much better it looks in my house. It brings stupid ideas to my mind of keeping Willow around. We could make it work living out here together. She's already made this place into a far better home than I ever could. My heart rate spikes at the thought of having Willow forever.

First we need to survive a full day together.

Before those thoughts take root, Willow breaks my concentration. "Do you have anything to eat other than steak and beans?" She asks as she searches through the mostly empty cabinets. Her question reminds me that I haven't had any food since yesterday afternoon.

I mentally list the scarce options as I head toward her. "There might be some random crap in the freezer. I'm due for a delivery soon so the choices are very limited." I rest against the table and secretly appreciate her position. She's stretching tall to reach a can of soup and I have to suppress a groan at how fucking hot she looks.

"Random crap? Xander, you seriously need to take better care of yourself. I'm surprised you've survived this long." Her voice is laced with humor but she doesn't realize how close to truth her words are. I've had some very close calls but not for the reasons she's currently insinuating.

She faces me and I shrug my shoulders. I know Willow is trying to lighten the mood but I'm not sure how to joke around anymore. It reminds me how little she knows me.

She takes my silence the wrong way, of course. "You're not sneaking back in your shell, Xander. No way. You told me we would talk. Don't you dare shut me out." There is a hint of whine in her tone that I remember extremely well. I always gave in and Willow used it to get her way.

I scrub my hands over my face and try not to get frustrated. I have a feeling we will have countless misunderstandings until I can figure out how to communicate like a normal person again. This time I let the groan escape before trying to explain myself.

"I'm not going back on my word, Willow. Sometimes I don't know what to say. As you've figured out, I don't have any desire to spend time with people so my social skills are rusty. It hasn't mattered until now. I didn't know how to respond to your teasing." I let out an exasperated sigh at having to admit my shortcomings again.

"Let's eat quick and then we can take a walk. Did you find the beef jerky?"

Willow's lips spread into a wide smile. I almost fucking sway on my feet from the sight.

"Jerky? Now you're talking. See? Not everything has changed." She sounds way too excited about that but at least she's happy again.

For now.

nineteen

willow

I've been silently freaking out waiting for Xander to be ready for our discussion. I don't expect him to open up about everything but I would love for at least a few blanks to be filled. While he was showering, I finished cleaning and attempted to make dinner for us. The problem with that plan was the serious lack of food in this house. It was one more thing that made me really rattled about Xander's situation.

When he joined me in the kitchen, it took colossal strength to keep the smile on my face. It was even more difficult to appear unaffected after everything that has happened today. It has seriously been the most intense afternoon of my life and it keeps getting crazier.

When I thought he was pushing me away again, I got a little defensive before downplaying my raging emotions. I went overboard with the beef jerky. Xander probably thinks I'm losing my marbles and he wouldn't be far off.

I'll be so relieved if he lowers his guard enough for us to truly know each other again. I won't be so moody and unstable around him once we have more common ground. That is what bothers me the most about all of this, as selfish as that sounds. I desperately miss my best friend and I want our connection back. Obviously I want so much more than that but I figure we can start slow. If we can build the trust back, maybe I'll be comfortable finally confessing my love for him.

Maybe I'm being too pushy and forward with my actions but if I'm not, Xander would probably go back to total isolation. I cannot let that happen. Even though all this unpredictability it's making me mental, I can tell I'm helping him by being here.

I'm standing outside while Xander finishes whatever he's doing inside. I'm eager to get going and hopefully resolve some of this excessive stress that is constantly bubbling under my skin. The barriers between us are problematic but our connection is stronger. I need to be patient though our status is complicated and complex. For starters, I didn't even know how long I was invited to stay.

I look up as Xander slams the door and stomps down the rickety steps. Once he's by my side, I can practically see the nerves rippling off him. What a perplexing pair we make. Both of us all flustered and hectic since we no longer have the effortless ease between us.

"Where to, boss man?"

Boss man? Seriously?

Face meet palm. I'm internally bashing myself as soon as the words are out of my mouth but I've always owned my quirks. Xander used to like that about me. My goofiness only gets worse when I'm worried, which is probably some unconscious coping strategy. Xander better speak up and save me from myself.

He snorts and shakes his head.

Maybe I broke the tension a bit.

"Let's head that way." He waves his hand toward some random destination over his left shoulder. "There's a path to a place I think you'll enjoy."

We stand there for an awkward moment, neither of us making the first move. I stare up into his amazing blue eyes and wait him out. Soon enough Xander steps out of the way and motions me forward.

Such a gentleman. I can only hope he'll check out my butt while he's back there.

My inner monologue is so cheesy as those ridiculous words scroll through my mind. I'm startled out of my musings when Xander clasps his hand around mine. Holy crap, I think my heart is about to beat out of my chest. He actually initiated contact! This is huge. What does this mean?

I'm going to overanalyze the crap out of this.

I try to take a sneak peek at Xander out of the corner of my eye but he's already looking my way. My entire body heats up as tingles spread from head to toe. I feel the traitorous pink blossom on my cheeks, efficiently exposing my sheer delight. I'm so giddy over such a simple gesture but I've been waiting years for Xander to causally hold my hand.

"Is this okay?" He asks while holding our joined hands up. He sounds so vulnerable and stares at me with such longing. He's being honest and open, which shines from his stunning irises. It causes a swarm of butterflies to erupt in my belly.

I'm nodding like a fool before I can get the words out. "Yes. Of course. I like it a lot, Xander." My voice is a breathy rasp that belongs in the bedroom. Gosh, I'm a hot mess. At least he doesn't catch on to my giddy-girl struggle. I need to get my head in the game because this is all about Xander.

It's hard to tell with all that facial hair in the way but I swear a ghost of a smile just graced Xander's lips. Tears blur my vision momentarily at the flurry of emotion this man has been revealing today. My long-kept secret almost bursts from my lips but I clamp my jaw shut. Instead I focus on supporting him through this awful stage of traumatic grief.

Our boots crunch through the snow as we continue on our expedition. White decorates almost every surface, which creates an angelic setting. It matches the soothing silence that can only be found far from the city. It is very beautiful and peaceful. I can definitely see the appeal of living out here. I appreciate the natural beauty surrounding us from all sides. Xander could be using the expansive wilderness to hide but I hope he's getting more out of it than that.

We duck under a few trees and cut through some rough terrain before Xander pulls me to a stop. He's brought me to a type of clearing in the center of the woods and it takes my breath away for a moment.

The trees provide shelter from the elements so the ground is fairly free of winter slush. Colorful leaves decorate the forest floor and it reminds me of a fall themed rainbow. A narrow stream flows nearby and offers a delicate acoustic tone. It all molds together to create the perfect escape from harsh reality. I totally get it. If I were a photographer, I would dedicate an entire exhibit just to this serene space.

Xander releases my hand and steps over to a large shrub. I miss the connection instantly. He pulls a chair from under the branches and shakes off the debris. That's super random but a perfect topic to begin a discussion.

"Xander, this place is amazing. Seriously. Do you come out here often? And what's with the chair?" I stammer slightly, since I'm not sure what to expect.

He plops the seat down and motions for me to sit.

"I consider this my solace. It's a great spot to collect my runaway thoughts and just be still for awhile. I get a semblance of normal. If I have to discuss uncomfortable shit, I would prefer being somewhere I like." Xander's tone already holds an edge and I'm concerned about his willingness to share much.

"This doesn't have to be a huge deal. I didn't mean to put pressure on you. I really think talking about it will help but you don't need to tell me anything." I can tell he's anxious and I want to soothe his nerves, yet I really want him to push past these barriers so we can move forward.

"We can start slow, Xander. Let's not talk about the army or your time overseas. Obviously that's too much. Will you tell me about your tattoo?" I ask the question easily. I could be opening a painful can of worms by asking but I'm dying of curiosity.

When my words register, Xander's face pales and his mouth gapes slightly. As though it's an absolute surprise I want to know about his ink of all things. I thought it was a safe subject to address but maybe not. He should be aware of my burning need to know why he chose that skillfully gnarled tree. My body hums with fire as I recall the tangled pattern adorning his immaculate right side.

Xander fidgets uncomfortably for a second, his hands curling into tight fists before easing open again. His forehead furrows as a grimace covers his face. His lips open a few times as if to speak but then he closes them again. It's all up to him and what he wants to admit.

He takes a deep breath in preparation and forces a loud exhale past his lips. Xander tips his face toward the sky before pulling the pin from the grenade.

"The design is a tribute to the only girl I've ever loved."

twenty

xander

Once I confess the truth about my tattoo, I know it's the right choice. A huge weight has lifted off my straining shoulders. That is until Willow starts choking.

Her top half folds over her legs as she gasps for breath. Thankfully she doesn't fall out of the chair. I approach her slowly to offer a pat on the back but she wildly swats me away with the hand not clutching her throat.

I knew if I didn't blurt out my secret, I wouldn't tell Willow. It would continue to be one of the many roadblocks separating us. I just didn't anticipate she'd react quite so strongly.

I stand back and watch her struggle for a few minutes. It gives me a chance to evaluate our complicated shit. I know how closed off and guarded I am but I'm not opposed to letting her hang around. Not anymore. I enjoy Willow's company too much already and I don't want to send her packing. It'll come back to bite me but I couldn't care less right now.

My focus remains on Willow's heaving form as she slows her breathing. She lifts her head to glare at me and I notice tears in her eyes.

Fuck. Were those caused from emotions or the hacking?

"What the *heck*, Xander? How do you just toss that declaration out willy-nilly? Seriously? You barely freaking talk to me and now you're confessing something like that?!" Willow spits the words out like they taste bad. I can't remember a time she's ever been mad like this.

She leaps from her seat and begins pacing frantically. Her hands flail about as she continues her rant. "I don't even know what to say. How do I respond to that, Xander? I'm so freaking frustrated with you! I mean, why didn't you tell me before? Why?" Willow's steps abruptly stop and she turns to face me.

"Wait. The design is a willow tree, right? I'm not making wild assumptions right? Holy crap, Xander. Tell me I'm not being crazy!" Her eyes glow as they widened in horror.

Damn, she's so fucking sexy.

How could there ever be anyone but her? I've been obsessed with her since we were in middle school. We were always together and I guzzled down every drop of attention she gave me. My eyes were constantly tracking her whenever she was near. My heart sped up as she would approach me. The words that would have explained my feelings were never said but she could have figured it out.

Since Willow has been staying with me, she is all I think about. She's the reason the fucking ghosts have stopped haunting me incessantly. Bright light has gracefully infiltrated my pitch-black existence and I'll never be able to repay her for bringing me back from the ledge.

Can she seriously think I had some other girl in mind when I got my tattoo? I have to end that ridiculous train of thought right the fuck now.

I close the distance between us in a few long strides. When I'm close enough to touch, I gave her more honesty. "I think you know the answer to that, Willow. You're not being crazy, unless you actually believe I'd admit to loving someone else." My voice is gruff yet soft.

I can't stop from touching her in some small way. I gently push some hair from her face and caress her cheek with the back of my fingers when I pull away. Willow trembles and peers up at me from under her lashes. She better not try getting shy on me now.

"I've never been good with expressing how I feel and I'm really shit at it now. Just know, even through all the pain and suffering, you were always with me as a reminder. On my darkest days, your memory was there to yank me back from the breaking point," I whisper against her lips. Willow's breathe stutters as she sways in my grasp.

She sucks at the corner of her mouth and the tease is enough to snap my restraint.

I crush my mouth to hers while hooking my hands under her thighs. In the next instant, I have WIllow's back against a nearby tree as I eagerly stroke her tongue with mine. Our bodies fit together effortlessly, which only adds to my rapidly building arousal. Willow is everything I've been missing these past three years.

We're fueled purely by desire for several moments. Clutching fingers, rocking hips, and panting moans. I'm quickly getting absorbed into this woman as my body melds with hers. Willow is silky and soft in contrast to my jagged edges so the combination is fucking electric. I never want the heat under my skin to quit burning.

Just when I think Willow wants me to fuck her in these woods, she pushes against my shoulder and withdraws her mouth from our heated connection.

Damn.

"Wait. Hold on a second, Xander. I want to hear the story." Her tone holds a hint of a groan as I rock into her.

She wants to talk?

Now?

"What story?" I ask while sucking her earlobe between my teeth. Willow leans into me and digs her heels into my ass. Maybe I can convince her to give up the chitchat.

Willow pulls away from me again even though I attempt to keep her locked in my embrace. "The tattoo. I want the details. You're not getting out of this. No matter how tempting the alternative." Her stare reflects her unwavering determination.

My forehead drops to her shoulder as I exhale a loud sigh, trying to cool the fuck down. Damn, this girl has all the control but I couldn't really care less. Willow owns my sorry ass.

I unwind her legs from my hips and slowly ease her to the ground. I drop a chaste kiss to her lips before stepping out of her hold. I scratch at my beard and fidget with the hem of my shirt. I can't stall forever.

"All right. I don't think there's much to share but you can be the judge." I've never been able to talk to anyone about my time overseas but telling Willow doesn't seem like such a huge undertaking.

I take a deep breath and continue, "Being deployed really sucked, especially at first. There isn't a way to explain it to someone that hasn't experienced it, but just know I had a really tough time adjusting.

"Everything is so fucking different over there. It's lonely and scary and you never know what could happen. Living through that shit changes you. I tried so damn hard to stay strong, especially for you, but there were times I wanted to give up.

"Before I bonded with the guys in my troop," my throat locks up at the mention of my fallen brothers. It makes my chest constrict but I grit my teeth and push past it. "I was by myself a lot. I thought about you constantly, Willow. I would close my eyes and picture you. I don't know why I never told you how I felt. It seems so fucking foolish now. Maybe things could have been different."

I sound fucking defeated even though Willow is standing right in front of me. I suppose it still doesn't seem possible.

Will I ever believe she wants to be here willingly?

Willow looks like a fallen angel that I've corrupted. Leaves are scattered in her chocolate hair but the strands still shine in the sun. Her plump lips are swollen and tempting me to ditch story time, but her beautiful green eyes are pleading with me to keep going. I'm a slave to her silent demand so I comply easily.

"One stupid night, a group of us went out drinking. I got shitfaced and that just made me miss you even more. I started jabbering on about you and one of my friends put the idea in my head to get some ink. It sounded like a good plan and I knew exactly what I wanted.

"I've shown you plenty of my random drawings over the years but never the ones dedicated to you. I have pages filled with willow trees and different things that remind me of you. Since I was a sappy shit, I carried around a favorite piece. We strolled into the parlor, I handed the paper over, sat down, and the artist went to work."

I swallow hard at the memory of the dull ache the needle caused while digging into my skin. I recall smirking like a tool imagining Willow's reaction when she discovered my ultimate commitment. The reality was drastically opposite. I shove my hands deep into my pockets and find the courage to finish this.

"I woke up the next morning with a killer hangover and my entire right side was throbbing. When I looked at the tattoo, I smiled for the first time in weeks."

"I sound like such a loser but it made me feel like you were there with me, Willow. In the worst place on Earth, I had a radiant companion by my side, keeping me safe.

"It doesn't seem like it but I was still relying on you, on the memory of you, every single day. Until you showed up. It's messed up because I treated you like shit but I didn't know how to handle actually seeing you again. The past several days have been a disaster but I don't regret anything because you're still here." I clear my throat after the final word. My guts have been spilled all over this forest so I'm feeling pretty damn vulnerable.

I sound like a pussy-whipped bitch but I'll accept the repercussions. I won't give her a watered down version. She wants to hear the truth so she better be able to handle it.

Willow is quietly assessing me and my chest begins to tighten as the anxiety creeps in. There is a dull throb piercing through my skull and tremors cause my fingers to shake. The gates I just opened are threatening to slam shut. I don't want to regret my words but I'm beginning to wonder if I went too far. I don't know what I'll do if she rejects my dumbass.

While I'm busy warring with myself, Willow finally speaks, and her question is the one I've been dreading.

twenty-one

willow

"Why didn't you write me, Xander?"

The entire time he was speaking, I kept circling back to the same freaking question. If he cared so much, missed me *so* terribly, then why didn't he contact me?

The day we parted three years ago burns brightly in my mind.

He promised me.

To find out he constantly thought of me yet didn't reach out, pours salt in my open wounds.

Xander stands motionless in front of me for several moments after the question leaves my mouth. If he knows me at all, which he dang well should, he knew that question was coming. I waited for those letters daily but they never came. No correspondence of any kind. The distance between us emotionally slowly began to match the physical space. It broke my heart but I wasn't in control of it. I had no address or way to contact him. Xander needed to reach out first and he never did.

Don't get me wrong, I went all mushy inside for a hot minute when Xander admitted his long time affection. But then confusion plowed over the joy and my brain was scrambled over the stunning admission just laid at my feet. I'm so baffled, the moment I've been waiting for–for years–has a tainted hue.

Xander loved me? That news has a chorus of angels, serenading me with heavenly hymns, taking up real estate in my soul. I am freaking ecstatic.

Xander loved me but not connecting with me for three years? Yeah, I want to go bang my head against the nearby tree. I think about all the wasted chances that I let slip by as well, which only makes me feel worse.

Usually I'm very patient and understanding, but right now unease bubbles in my stomach. My ears are ringing and a strain is pulling at my neck. Lover not a fighter? Right now, I want to say screw being nice by avoiding tough topics. I want to dive right in and discover why we allowed this to happen. I won't though. I might be crushed and disappointed, but more than anything, I'm scared to take it out on Xander.

He nervously shuffles his feet as he pushes his fists deeper into his pockets. "Right for the jugular, Willow? You couldn't comment on my feelings first? Then dig into how I fucked up?" His defensive tone makes me feel really guilty but I'm fueled by my need to know more.

I shake my head, afraid my voice will betray me. He knows what I want. I don't need to repeat myself. I try to shake off the animosity. I allow my eyes to slowly rake over Xander's enormous body.

Darn, he's hard to resist when he's all tense and coiled tight.

His eyes are like blue flames that want to consume me. I

can't stop the heat from pooling in my belly.

Maybe Xander was expecting me to fall helplessly into his arms and swoon all over his enticing words but I was thrown way off course. I had no idea he felt this way for me, after all this time. The shock reverberates through my bones and it causes a shudder to roll through me.

How did we let this happen?

Why didn't we tell each other sooner?

The unknowns keep bouncing through my head but I become distracted by Xander's brooding sexiness. I shake off the heat spreading through my veins. He can be smoldering hotness all he wants but we are finishing this dang conversation.

I tilt my head and catch a glimpse of the Xander I used to know, hiding underneath all that appetizing muscle. I expected him to be different, of course. No one comes back from war unaffected but anyone would describe Xander's transformation as extreme. Being able to see a piece of the boy I grew up with has my heart beating erratically. I've obsessed about finding a connection to the past since stumbling upon the detached version of him so the relief consumes me now.

As my question continues to hang unanswered, my silent scrutiny of Xander triggers a memory from before he was deployed. It flashes into my mind, resurfacing an opposite version of this man, and whisks me away to the comforting past.

I heard him before I saw him. Xander always knew where to find me when I was upset. It was like a sixth sense between us.

He settled on the swing next to me and gently started rocking.

"Remember when we first met? At this park? The summer I moved here?" Xander asks questions in rapid succession as a way to distract me. It's sweet that he tries so I go along with it.

I join in the recollection. "You were such a cute little kid. All lanky limbs and floppy hair. I knew we would make great friends."

"And look at us now, Wills."

I turn to him and Xander is flashing a brilliant smile at me. He's so hot. I can hardly handle our close friendship some days.

"Just as I predicted. Right as always." *I chuckle when he scoffs at my response.*

"So, what brings you out here today?"

I'm not surprised he's ready to solve the issue.

I sigh and bury my shoe in the wood chips. "I went on a date with Doug Nelson and it didn't go very well."

Xander cringes. "I told you not to bother with that loser. He's such a jackass on the field and I'm surprised Coach puts up with him. What did he do?"

"I tried not getting my hopes up. I'd heard all about his reputation but the naive girl inside me didn't believe the rumors. All he wanted was sex. It was obvious from the moment he picked me up." *I knew my tone was bitter. I didn't care about Doug or the stupid date. My pride was injured when he assumed I'd just sleep with him.*

Xander makes a strange noise that sounds like a growl. It sounded funny coming from him. "What a douche. You shouldn't be wasting your time on jerks like that, Wills. You need to find a guy that will treat you with respect. You deserve so much better."

"Oh yeah, X? Where am I going to find a guy like that? All I catch are horny boys looking to score." *I set a trap I knew he wouldn't fall into. I've been secretly in love with him since we were thirteen but I could never find the guts to tell him.*

Xander seems to ponder my options before simply saying, "me." *He shrugs his shoulders and gives me another huge smile.*

What is happening right now?

Does he actually mean that?

His laughter breaks up my mini meltdown. "You should see your face, Wills. It looks like you've seen a ghost. Don't freak out or anything. I was joking. The right guy will come around eventually. Just enjoy yourself. We're too young to stress about that crap." *His fluffy statements hurt my heart, even though they shouldn't.*

We're just friends.

My feelings for him are far from platonic.

I love him. Xander is the one I truly want.

Why doesn't he love me too?

Xander gently touches my shoulder and shakes me a bit. "Relax. Let's go get ice cream. That always makes you feel better. I'll even pay." His dimples come out in full force and I lose my breath.

Why does he have to be so freaking perfect?

"Willow?" The sound of my name brings me back to the present.

"You seem a thousand miles away. Maybe we should talk about this later." Xander's voice is laced with concern.

He puffs out a mouthful of air and I take a moment to digest his masculine beauty. He is so darn sexy, yet I'm still unsure where we're headed from here. I so badly want to rewind the clock and confess my love for him before he left. How could that have changed things?

An overwhelming wave of misery crashes over me as I picture a collection of lost moments. The days we could have spent cuddling on the beach. The nights we would have enjoyed wrapped around each other. Stolen kisses and lingering touches. I desperately want those memories but they vanish before my eyes. A deep inhale fills my lungs as I process through my pain.

"No. I want to know, Xander. I need to hear this." I try to keep the bubbling hurt from my voice. My chin begins to tremble so I cover the offending twitch with my palm. Xander takes notice of my distress and swoops in closer.

I use my free hand to wave him off. "Tell me, Xander. I want to know."

Darn it, my eyes are watering.

I'm such a mess. Emotional overload is not a joke.

Xander takes pity on me and begins another section to our broken history. "I know how much I fucked up, all right? I promised to write. I swore I would call. All you got was silence. I'm a piece of shit for that, WIllow. I deserve the fury in your beautiful eyes. I own the hurt you're tossing my way." He chokes on the words like they are tough to say. I realize too late that he's not used to communicating at all, yet I'm forcing him to divulge painful experiences.

"You need to try and understand what a horrible situation I was thrown into. Even though I thought of you practically every moment of almost everyday, I didn't know how to express that on paper. Each time I tried, my hand would start shaking uncontrollably. I'd get frustrated that I was being affected so severely by that place."

His rugged face becomes tense as the struggle he went through flashes through his ocean eyes. Weariness is displayed by his sunken cheeks and dark circles under his eyes. Xander's eyebrows bunch together as he keeps delving deeper into the story.

"I wanted to call, Willow. The sound of your voice was sure to soothe even my most fucked up nerves but I couldn't dial the numbers. It seemed like I was protecting you from knowing how awful my life was over there. I tricked myself into believing it was better that way. I didn't want to drag you down. I wanted to keep you innocent and sweet and naive. I didn't do it to be an asshole, although I realize that is exactly how it came across. I promise you that wasn't my intention. I've only wanted what was best for you, Willow. I didn't want that shit to touch you.

"My plan was to do my stint there and come back to you. Then we could start again. I could describe my every desire to your face rather than in a hurried letter. *Fuck.* I get it, Willow. My mistakes are stacked against me and I don't have a way past them. You gave me fucking hope that perhaps it wasn't irreparable but now I'm worried you're ready to tuck tail. I wouldn't blame you, but I'm not sure I can let you leave."

He sucks in a deep breath and aims his chin to the treetops.

His fingers rake through his shaggy hair and yank at the ends. Xander is beginning to crumble and my soul instantly wants to provide him with comfort. He did as I asked. He told me the honest truth, even though it rubbed me wrong. I have to give him credit for trying to shield me in his own warped way.

"Xander, I won't lie to you. I really suffered from not hearing from you. You were my best friend and you always had my back. I never expected you to leave and forget about me. I mean, I suppose I should be thankful you tried keeping me separate from your life over there. But, I'm really sad that you didn't think of how your silence would affect me." My voice wobbled as I lost the fight against my tears. They began freely flowing down my cheeks but I continued talking.

"I wanted to support you. I knew it wouldn't be easy. I understood that you would have plenty of baggage to bring back with you but I would've helped carry the weight. Instead I got nothing. That hurt worse, Xander. And now? Knowing how you truly felt about me? I don't know what to do. Maybe I should go." I can hardly see through my bleary eyes but I notice when Xander swings his furious face my way.

He storms close enough to touch me, yet doesn't. The fire is back in his blazing eyes but I have a feeling the heat is fed by fury. His jaw is clenched and the familiar growl is gurgling in his throat.

"No! You need to stay. Fuck that shit, Willow. You can't leave. No, no, no. Let's hash it out but don't fucking go. *SHIT!*" He spins around and begins pacing, again. The panic mixed with rage doesn't make a great combination. Xander's racing off the rails.

He pounds his fist into the trunk of a tree and howls out as the wood splinters. Xander's knuckles are bleeding as he stomps back to me. I take a step back, unsure what to expect.

He stops in his tracks and lowers his head. His chest rises and falls quickly with his labored breathing.

"Are you afraid of me, Willow?" His hushed voice comes

out between pants.

Crap.

I hate that Xander's impulsive assumption is that I'm scared of him. That really wasn't the case. I step forward to close the distance between us.

"Look at me," I hush out quietly, trying to soothe his tattered mind. Xander lifts his wounded eyes and guilt swallowed me in one gulp. I felt like such a brat.

"I didn't step back out of fear. I think you can understand I'm a little on edge. I wasn't sure what you needed right then. Did you need more space? Were you going to push up against me again? I backed away because of the unknown. I promise, Xander. I'm full of a lot of mixed emotions, like confusion and hurt, but I could never be frightened of you." I hope my explanation is enough.

He speaks low and faint. "Alright. I'm sorry I freaked out just now. I can't handle the thought of you leaving, even though you probably should be running away right now. Please don't, Willow. I need you. I'm doing a shitty fucking job showing it but you're helping me. I need you to stay."

I'm sure it takes a lot for him to admit that, and it proves how vital my presence is here. My professional side understands how his growing dependence on me could be seen as an issue, but to me, it's a messed up way of rebuilding our bond. We were always inseparable growing up. I didn't see this as *that* different.

I place my palm on his scruffy cheek and my heart leaps when he leans into my touch.

"I need you too, Xander. This entire day has been chaotic and I'm sorry if I gave you the impression I would leave. When I said I should go, I meant for a little walk or something. I want to stay with you, Xander. I'm glad you want me here, too." When I finish, I shift forward a stitch to press a delicate kiss on his lips. When I pull back, warmth is reflected in Xander's eyes.

He releases a long sigh before whispering, "Thank you."

After a few collective moments, Xander asks a solid question. "So, now what?"

"How about ice cream? It always makes me feel better." A warm smile graces my lips as I make the past our present.

twenty-two

xander

I can't believe this shit.

My head is throbbing as I clutch it between my palms in an attempt to shut down the persistent badgering. The constant pounding in my skull won't fucking quit.

I can't concentrate, definitely can't sleep, and I'm stressed as fuck that the voices are going to start back up.

Since I'm a fucking wimp, I'm currently holed up in the shed in order to keep a bit of distance between us. These commanding urges are persuading me back to the house but I stamp them down with the last of my control. Practically every piece of me believes hiding out here is a horrible idea and my mind is quickly losing the battle.

I'm trying to stay fucking strong but the pull is powerful.

When Willow and I got back after our time in the woods, I wasn't sure what to do. Thankfully I didn't have to panic for long.

She provided me with an escape by taking a shower. I used the lull to gather my tattered thoughts. Then the water blasted on and I began picturing Willow getting naked. It was too fucking close to my fantasy the other day.

My entire body was locked up tight. I was tense, agitated, and sweating as the chaos from our evening continued spinning. I hated being out of control. Spending the night separated from her would be best for both of us.

I waited in the kitchen until Willow was out of the bathroom. As soon as she emerged, I stammered out my plan and practically sprinted out of the house. I didn't miss pinch of her eyebrows and the frown marring her gorgeous face but I couldn't handle exposing more of my demented shit than I already had.

The hallucinations and nightmares are the worst. I usually wake up worn the fuck out, so I probably thrash around like mad. I never want to know what that insanity looks like to a spectator.

Now it's the middle of the fucking night and I've been lying here wide-awake for hours.

Obsessing.

Panicking.

Conflicted.

Overreacting.

Tormented.

Irritated.

Freaking the fuck out.

I'm shocked the darkness hasn't come for me yet but I figure it's only a matter of time. The more drained and exhausted I am, the easier it is for the haunting shit to take over. I'm trying like hell to refuse my incessant infatuation with Willow.

She is going to leave me, just like everyone else, which is what I deserve. I'm destined to be alone but I want to give in and feel her warmth. Even for a little while.

I'm weak and pathetic.

I'm not capable of staying away. It goes against every instinct inside me. I'm fucking cursed and Willow is determined to screw up my resistance. I desperately crave the calm Willow injects into my system. I predicted this unhealthy attachment after she touched me yesterday. She is slowly, but very surely, dismantling all the protective defenses I've sufficiently been using.

In addition to the driving need to be near her, I have an irrational fear that something terrible will happen to Willow. Since I've been lowering my guard and letting her see my truth, I can't stop the hounding feeling nipping at my heels that she will get taken away from me. I'm going out of my mind compiling the potential threats that could harm her. I won't be able to rest until I know she's fine.

As I make my way across the frozen yard, I'm negotiating terms with this madness.

If she actually fucking listened to me and locked the door, I'll take it as a sign that she wants to keep the danger out. Including me. I can't get a handle on my nerves as I march up the porch steps. When I reach the door, a lungful of air escapes me as I take a moment to hope the knob turns. My trembling hand makes me realize how desperate I am to get inside. When my palm is able to twist the cool metal, I'm so fucking relieved I almost forget to snap the deadbolt behind me.

It's difficult to see across the small space but I know my way around. With a few long strides, I am looming over Willow's sleeping form.

Her legs are twisted together like a pretzel, while her left arm appears bent at an awkward angle. Willow's face is partially hidden by a pillow but I can tell she's breathing normally. I wonder how she can be comfortable that way.

My racing heart settles knowing Willow is safe.

Now what the fuck am I going to do?

I stand around like a moron as I contemplate my options.

There's no way I can go back to the shed. I don't trust myself to lay next to Willow so I take a seat on the floor near the bed.

My head is resting against the edge of the mattress and my mind easily drifts. Just as I'm starting to doze off, I get the most exquisite sensation and goosebumps cover my flesh as Willow's thigh rubs against my head.

"Why don't you lay down with me?" Willow's voice is groggy and sexy as fuck. I want to drag my tongue along her throat to feel the vibrations when she speaks.

Instead I grunt, "I have my reasons."

"I wish you'd tell me, Xander. I've always been here for you. We just got interrupted for a while."

I make another noncommittal noise. Interrupted? More like blown to unrecognizable pieces because of my stupid mouth.

Her fingers resume their ministrations and I hum in approval. Tingling sparks erupt on every surface of my body. My fingers twitch with the desire to return the favor. It feels so good that I almost fall asleep again.

I could definitely get used to this.

The errant thought shocks my system and I'm instantly alert. I can't get comfortable with what I'm sure is a temporary situation. Willow is going to leave and take any progress I've made with her. With that simple thought, my entire being is drowning in sorrow and air gets trapped in my clogged throat. Startling chills shoot up my spine as my veins fill with ice. Willow has become my fucking lifeline and I can't exist without her. Maybe I can persuade her to stay. I try to use that appealing approach to calm the fuck down. At least she's here for now.

As if hearing my silent struggle, Willow whispers out a quiet, "Xander?"

"Yeah?" My tone is hushed too.

"Will you tell me a story from the time you were gone? It doesn't have to be anything significant. Anything you want to share. Maybe from a day that wasn't so bad, if one even exists." With her words, my mood plummets again.

I hate fucking thinking about that time in my life. Usually I hyperventilate. A good memory from that shit hole? Not likely. I don't want to let her down but *fuck*.

After digesting her request a little more, a blip of something not totally rancid registers. I could tell her about the first camp I was stationed at before shipping out to the desert. That's where I met Corporal Jones and we ended up getting along pretty well. At least for the short time I was held at that temporary holding point.

I'm not sure what happened to Jones since he stayed back when we all left. We didn't have the close bond I shared with my fellow squad mates, but I would consider him a friend.

"All right, maybe this will be decent. When I first arrived in Europe, we stayed at a base in Germany. That's a typical landing spot to gather before heading off to the next location. There was this soldier I bunked near that ended up being really funny. Corporal Jones was on his second tour and had all kinds of advice to give a newbie like me." I took a deep breath and decided which hilarious thing to share with Willow.

If I were still the same man I was then, I would be busting a gut recalling all the goofy crap Jones spewed. Even with the gains I've recently made, the corners of my lips hardly twitch.

"One night, Jones was filling us in on a mission he carried out when he first enlisted. He was out in the middle of fucking no man's land with his entire unit for this covert operation. They had to hide out for several days at a time without returning to the command post for supplies. In those situations, soldiers can get desperate and extremely creative.

"On this specific excursion, their troop was attacked and under fire from the enemy forces. No one was injured but Jones shit his pants, which he never lived down. He had to strip down behind a boulder to remove his soiled briefs. Fatigues are rough and easily chafe sensitive skin so going without a layer between is dicey. What choice did he have though? From that point on, Jones wore an extra set just in case. The moral of the story is you truly never know what the fuck is going to happen out there so be prepared for anything. Including unexpected bowel movements. His whole point was to bring an extra pair of clean underwear. Not about watching your back while you're being shot or always be ready for an ambush, but rather make sure to have clean fucking underwear. When he told us that, I almost peed my fucking shorts. Damn, that guy was a riot."

It seems like I rambled on for hours even though I know it has only been a few minutes. Willow's hand in my hair stilled and I'm sure the sandman caught her. She probably didn't hear most of that but it wasn't horrible reminiscing about that moment. It actually felt pretty good. Maybe Willow is onto something.

When she suddenly breaks the eerie quiet, I almost jump out of my fucking skin.

"Thank you for that. Jones sounds like a funny dude." She sounds half asleep but I guess she stuck with me until the end.

I lay my head back down against the bed and close my tired eyes. There aren't any voices screaming in my ears or gruesome images dancing in my vision. A calming balm seeps into my skin as a sense of peace washes over me.

Maybe I can survive this shit after all.

twenty-three

willow

I wake up the same way I have the past two mornings since I've been staying with Xander. I'm conflicted and a little frustrated as I rub my bleary eyes.

Xander still refuses to sleep in bed with me so he's leaning against the mattress from his spot on the floor. My hand is buried in his hair, my body is curled around his head, and my legs are hanging over his left shoulder. This definitely isn't the most practical position but I've gotten used to it. I've accepted that Xander won't spend the night any closer than this. For now.

The biggest problem I'm currently dealing with is my raging hormones. I'm so freaking horny because I'm constantly assaulted with Xander's sexiness. He's driving me wild with lust but isn't rushing to ease my desperate ache. I think drastic measures are in order.

Don't get me wrong, the last forty-eight hours have been

fantastic. Once Xander told me about Jones, he found plenty of random stories to share. I heard a lot about the Corporal at first but then Xander found new subject matter. He willingly told a few tales about the soldiers from his unit but I could tell those were much harder to divulge. I'm totally blissed out that he's starting to trust me again.

I haven't forgotten about his tattoo or his admission of loving me. That was before he came back and we reunited so how does he feel now? I think we've left that topic alone for the time being and are just focusing on being near each other again.

I don't need a label or a serious commitment, at least not yet. It would be nice to be aware of his current thoughts and feelings though.

Is he keeping me around to stave off his darkness or is he hoping for more? Am I here strictly as his friend? Does Xander just see me as a screw buddy or is there relationship potential?

There is so much we need to discuss.

We had crazy hot sex but maybe that was a one time, heat of the moment, deal. Xander hasn't shown any interest in a repeat performance since our kiss in the woods. I've been dropping plenty of blatant hints but I get nothing in return.

When we sit on the couch, I've made sure to eagerly climb on his lap so we can snuggle close. He receives plenty of scorching kisses whenever the mood strikes me, which is *always*. When Xander gets undressed, I make sure to be extremely obvious that I'm checking out his fantastically ripped body. Aside from hopping on top and taking what I want, I've tried everything.

Our limited physical connections have been dynamite, clearly, but I'm discovering the complexity of my love for Xander all over again. Broken pieces and all.

I'm constantly driving myself mad obsessing over these details. The urge to get answers to these petty questions strengthens the more time I spend here. I've figured out what I want but

I have no clue what Xander is thinking. He's got a ton to deal with already.

I've noticed subtle signs of panic throughout the day, such as his eyes rapidly darting around the room searching for threats. A few times he's leapt from his chair and started pacing around manically, muttering under his breath. The good news is these instances have been happening less frequently the longer I've stayed but I still notice.

Xander is slowly opening up to me in ways he's comfortable with. I should happily accept the noticeable changes Xander has already made, and not put more pressure on him, but mixing in a little fun never hurt anyone. Especially if it benefits both of us.

He allowed me to take over his home and rearrange his personal belongings however I pleased. I wanted to try pushing the limits a few times by purposely doing stuff that used to drive Xander crazy. It makes me sound so rotten but I was desperate for him to unleash his passionate side again.

It was time to find a solution for this dry patch we've been lingering in. I stretch my tired limbs as I roll onto my back. My jerky movements wake Xander and he gradually begins shifting around. I toss out a loud groan for good measure and arch my back further. The shirt I'm wearing lifts up past my hips to expose my bare butt to the cool air. When I glance back at Xander, his focus is zoomed in on my naked skin. Turns out there is a definite benefit to running out of clean panties. This might be easier than I thought.

"Good morning." My voice rasps and sounds sultry even to my own ears. Upon hearing my words, Xander snaps his eyes away from my body before mumbling an unintelligible response.

I don't let that deter my plans. I bounce to the end of the mattress and slide my feet to the floor. I walk around to where Xander sits on the floor, making sure to add extra sway to my hips.

He tips his head up to look at me before lifting a brow

in question. "What's up, Willow? You look suspicious as hell."
Apparently nothing gets past this guy. Except all my previous,
extremely obvious, advances.

I pretend to be oblivious and casually shrug my shoulders.
"A shower sounds like a good way to start the day. After breakfast,
I figure I can finish the scarf I started yesterday unless you have
other ideas?"

Xander continues staring at me with a bland expression so
I turn away and sashay toward the bathroom. Halfway there, I
grip the bottom hem of my shirt and deliberately take my sweet
time taking it off.

A quick glimpse over my shoulder confirms Xander is watching my little striptease. A flirty grin lifts my lips as I walk over the
threshold and grip the doorknob. Xander's signature growl filters
across the space but I don't allow the sexy noise to distract me.

The water turns on with a hiss and I step back to let it
warm up. I look around the small room and wish the mirror was
intact. By this point, my appearance must be atrocious. Xander
only has the essentials, which does not include conditioner or a
brush. Don't get me started on the lack of moisturizer around
here. Thankfully, I'm not too high maintenance and I'd learned
to survive with far less while frequently camping over summer
weekends.

Once the steam starts rising, I hastily step under the stream.
I'm just getting my hair wet when the shower curtain is ripped
open. A shrill shriek slips from my throat even though I had been
hoping Xander would interrupt at any moment.

He looks furious but I recognize lust shining bright in his
blue eyes. "You think you can just sneak away after teasing me,
Willow? You won't get away with that shit."

Is he serious right now? I obviously wanted him to chase
me. I'll spell it out for him if that's what he needs. I take a small
step back so the water is no longer spraying my face.

I deliberately drag my tongue along my already wet lips. "I was hoping for some company in here. I'll wash your back if you wash mine."

Shock registers on his face. I'm not usually so bold but I'm done waiting.

"When did you become such a vixen? Tell the truth, Willow, you're not interested in getting clean. What you really want is to get dirty." Xander's tone hints at his arousal, which is confirmed when I check out the substantial bulge jutting out from his shorts.

All I could do was whisper, "yes."

The way Xander is staring at me heats my core past boiling. He seems ready to devour me as he trails his gaze along my naked flesh.

He doesn't hesitate once he jumps into the tub and backs me against the cool tiles. Before I can blink, Xander's head swoops down and his lips brutally meet mine. I graciously relax my jaw so his searching tongue can explore the depths of my mouth. Our parted lips are fused together and the intimate connection causes my heart to race.

Xander's slick chest easily slides along mine and the sensation against my nipples has me moaning into our kiss. I hate the fabric barrier between our hips and I desperately wanted it gone. My hands fly to the waistband of Xander's briefs with the intention of getting rid of them.

He separates from my lips to suck along my jaw. Once he's near my ear, he gently bites the lobe before muttering some straight sexiness.

"Are you aching? Do you need relief, Willow?" Xander's grumbled words momentarily distract me.

My charged response was immediate. "Oh my gosh, yes! Please, Xander. Don't make me wait." I rock into him so he'll know exactly how he was affecting me.

"I'm not going to fuck you, Willow. Not like this."

I freeze once his statement registers past the lust clouding my brain. Why the heck wouldn't he want sex? This better not be some stupid game or his way of getting back at me for taunting him.

He speaks again before I have a chance to ask what his problem is. "The next time I sink deep into your body, we'll be in my bed, where you belong. Then I can properly take care of you exactly how I've imagined worshipping you since I was a horny little boy."

Xander licks along my neck before continuing. I shiver in anticipation. "I'm still ashamed of what happened our first time and I won't do that rushed shit again. You're testing my good intentions and I almost want to say fuck it, but I won't do that again. No matter how fucking hot you are begging for it."

Dang, he knows how to reach me.

"Let's go then. I'm ready, Xander. I need you." I'm impatient and frantic and I know my voice comes out in a whine. Xander nips my skin before sucking the sting away.

"Not yet, Willow. I have plans and you're too worked up for me follow through with them. I'll ease your throbbing for now though. Don't fucking worry." As he speaks, his hand snakes between my thighs to emphasize his meaning. His fingers slip through my tingling slit and sparks ignite through my lower body. Xander alternates between biting, kissing, and sucking as he makes a path to my collarbone. He leans down so his mouth can feast on my breasts. Then he slips a nipple into his mouth and sucks. *Hard.* It feels so freaking amazing an aching throb hums through me, especially combined with his attention to my core.

His touch centers on my clit and spins rapid circles around the bundle of responsive nerves. The pulsing sensations are overwhelming and this is just from his fingers. My nails claw at his arms as I attempt to anchor myself to him through this intense pleasure.

When he eases a thick digit into my quivering center, I lose my breath on a gasp.

Holy crap.

I can't fathom anything better until he rubs the hidden spot no one has ever found. My legs tremble then my entire body starts to shake. I snap my eyes closed as the flames engulf me. This powerful orgasm has me soaring and reeling like I've never experienced before. I'm floating yet I feel heavy at the same time.

I lose track of time as the vibrations continue coursing through me. When I finally regain control, my unfocused gaze peers down at the man placing delicate kisses along my stomach.

As if feeling my stare, Xander looks at me before breaking me apart further. "Was that good for you, baby?" He's throwing around terms of endearment now? Xander is sprouting serious seeds within me that he wants me around for the long haul.

I run my fingers through his wet hair and let a relaxed smile lift my lips. I decide not to comment on the nickname in fear of ruining the moment.

The version of Xander I stumbled upon four days ago was already being a distant memory, and I was so thankful for that.

twenty-four
xander

Once Willow comes down from her climax, she tries returning the favor and even though I was fucking desperate to bury myself in her, I forced myself to wait until later. I shuck my shorts and take a legit shower with her.

Instead of getting off, I wash her back before she suds up mine. It's cheesy as hell but I couldn't give a shit. I love this girl and she's finally mine. I'm going to tell her tonight, no holding back.

When I called her baby, the shock registered on her expressive face and her reaction made me realize she was starving for more sweetness. Willow's eyes popped open wide as her breathing stalled so I dipped in for a quick kiss. The way her body melted into me was fucking paradise.

I can't deny how much she's already changed me. I want to be a better man because of her and believe I'm taking steps in the right direction.

Willow is breathing life back into my detached soul. She keeps the darkness away which makes it very easy to be around her. I'm gobbling up her light and basking in the fucking brightness. There's always the underlying worry that she's going to leave me, since I can't escape the awareness that she's eventually going to. For now, I do my best to push those depressing thoughts away since it makes my mood plummet instantly.

I feel like a bastard keeping Willow locked away out here. She's an outgoing person and always has been, so I'm positive there are plenty of people missing her right now. I bet she has a wonderful life back in the city but I want her all to myself. At least she hasn't brought up going back yet but she's dropped a few hints about specific things she's missing.

A big problem is her lack of clothing. I don't see the issue but Willow keeps talking about it. There is an old ass washing machine here that came with the house but I don't have a dryer. The clothes have to hang by the fire since it's the middle of winter, which takes so fucking long. She's been stuck wearing the same dirty shit over the past few days. She refuses to wear the previous day's panties so she's been going without. Again, I don't see the problem.

I really don't mind the fact that Willow has been sleeping in my shirts. It actually really fucking turns me on, which is why I suggested she put one on after our shower. I'll be uncomfortably rock hard all day just from staring at her but I guess that just makes me a glutton for punishment.

After we're dressed, I attempt making a decent breakfast for a change. Usually I eat whatever is quick and simple. I've never put too much thought into cooking. A slice of bread with some type of fruit was my typical morning meal but I want to do something special for Willow. Maybe it would help show that living here isn't so bad.

Thankfully, an order of groceries was delivered yesterday

so I have some decent options. I settle for the classic eggs, hash browns, and bacon combo. Willow raises a suspicious brow when she catches me whipping the yolks while trying not to burn the potatoes.

"Need any help? I don't have to sit here doing nothing, you know," she offers after noticing my glance in her direction.

A vision of us cooking together flits through my memory and reminds me of our past. It was something we often did together on the weekends when our parents weren't around. We were pretending to be adults by acting all domesticated but I never had a problem playing house with Willow.

Things might be drastically different now but I want that feeling back, so I agree without hesitation. "All right. How about you take over the eggs. Scrambled still good with you?"

Willow slides in close to me for access to the stove. She bumps into me with her hip before replying, "Of course." Then she scoffs like my question offended her before skidding back into her own space.

She's temptation fucking personified so I lean closer to lay a smack on her ass before grabbing a handful of the delectable flesh. Then I place a kiss on her cheek for good measure. When I pull back, I notice pink blossoming where my lips just were. Willow blushing over me is too fucking much. This woman is, without a doubt, going to be the end of me.

She clears her throat before speaking. "So, I've been meaning to ask you something." Her eyes flash to mine before quickly darting away. My gut clenches uncomfortably when I assume the worst.

She can't fucking leave me yet.

"Please hear me out before you refuse, okay?" Willow looks to me for confirmation and when I give a jerky nod, she continues, "You know I spoke with my mom last night. Well, she wanted me to ask if your mom could come out here to visit you."

I'm already shaking my head in the negative before she's done talking. "No way, Willow. No. I can't stand the thought of anyone else being here. I can't fucking do it." The panic starts to rise imagining my mother knocking on the door, trying to come in. I back away from the kitchen and begin anxiously stomping around the living room.

Willow turns off the burners and the room smells like spoiled crap. It reminds me of our breakfast that has now been ruined.

Fucking great.

Why did she have to bring this shit up? I had plans for us today and now I'm wound up so fucking tight my stomach hurts. I grab a nearby chair with the intention of hurling it across the room. Instead I slump down on the seat in a defeated heap.

With my head lowered, I don't see Willow approaching but I hear her light steps. Her warm grip on my shoulder brings relief to my panicked mind but it doesn't stop the maddening thoughts completely.

Guilt is seeping in because of my hostile reaction. This is my mother we are talking about, the woman that raised me. Not some fucking stranger. Why am I having such a difficult time seeing her? I'm sure my refusal has caused her a lot of pain. We used to be extremely close and now I can't handle having her in my house?

What the fuck.

I realize Willow has been speaking to me but I didn't catch any of it. Sounds like she's apologizing for upsetting me, which makes me feel even worse.

I'm such a piece of shit.

I interrupt her unnecessary explanation. "Stop saying you're sorry, Willow." My harsh tone causes her to suck in a sharp breath but it doesn't deter me. "There is nothing for you to feel bad about. This shit is on me. I'm the fuckup that can't stand the thought of people near me. All you did was make a request for someone that cares about me. I'm just having a tough time getting past my bullshit right now."

Willow gives my arm a squeeze before responding. "I understand, Xander. I didn't mean to upset you but I promised my mom I would at least ask."

A groan travels from my chest. "You didn't make me mad. Don't you dare take blame, Willow. I'm fucking frustrated with myself. I can't believe I thought I was making progress. Clearly I'm not capable of getting better. I'm fucking insane." I hear the growl rumble in my throat and it reminds me of the man that roared at Willow when she first arrived.

Fuck.

"Xander, stop. You are being way too hard on yourself. You've made such great strides these last few days. I'm so proud of you and I'm honored that you've allowed me to be here. You can't be so critical of your healing. You're the only one that knows your true limits and as long as you're trying to move forward, you're making improvements."

She's so calm and collected when she psycho-babbles. I don't mind in this case because her advice actually resonates with me. Willow has been an essential part of any growth I've managed to make. I owe her a lot and I don't want to disappoint her again.

The right fucking thing to do is let my mom come out here. After the way I acted the last time she tried to visit, I wasn't sure she would be willing to come back. Clearly I didn't scare her away permanently.

And honestly, I'm secretly pleased that my mom is sticking with me, even though my behavior toward her was repulsive. It would tear me apart if she actually gave up like I had demanded she do.

Willow hasn't said much for a few minutes, which is giving me with the opportunity to process through this shit. I feel trapped and I fucking hate it. I need to make the right choice and stop letting the anxiety control me.

I force the words out through my clenched jaw. "You can tell her to come out here. I'm not sure how I'll handle it once she's here but I need to at least try. She deserves better than a savage beast for a son." Thinking of how far I've fallen into the darkness brings a huge cloud of gloom over my already sour mood. If I head down this destructive path, I'm not sure I'll make it out. Thankfully Willow breaks apart my thoughts and disrupts my deprecation.

"Are you sure?" She pauses until I nod. "I hope you don't feel forced into this. I know how much it would mean to your mom though. I'll call and see when she can be out here. Maybe we could plan for tomorrow?" The idea of dealing with this mound of anxiety for that long makes my head throb.

I tell Willow exactly how I feel. "It needs to happen now. *Today.* I'm a wreck just thinking about it and I don't want to get fucking worse. If we're going to have my mom out here, I won't wait. Tell her that. She will make it work." I'm a selfish asshole but I refuse to struggle in agonized anticipation. The dread is already surging through my veins.

Willow rubs down my arm before returning her attention to my shoulder. I realize she's specifically touching skin covered in ink. It settles me slightly believing she's relishing my tattoo.

"Alright, Xander. I'll pass your message along. It'll all work out. Don't stress, okay? She only wants to spend time with you." Her voice is close to my ear and her warm breath feels good on my neck.

I turn my head so our foreheads touch. I don't fucking know what I'd do without Willow here. My eyes close as I release a long exhale.

"I appreciate everything you're doing for me. I hope you know that. Even though I'm terrible at telling you. I don't want my mom to get her hopes up too high. Can you fill her in on my fucked up mental situation? She can't stay out here. She doesn't expect that, right?" The panic swells until it begins to take over my thoughts.

Maybe this is a huge mistake.

Willow places her hand on my cheek and I lean into her touch. "I said don't stress, Xander. Your mom will be ecstatic with the fact you're open to having her visit. Even for a few moments. Trust me, she will be very understanding. You're in charge, all right?" Her words act as a balm to my erratic nerves. I like the idea of being in control, even though I know my demons really run the show.

I kiss Willow's palm before she pulls her hand away. Then I murmur a quiet, "All right."

Willow straightens and takes a step back. "Do you want to come with me while I make the call?"

"I can stay here. I'll clean up the kitchen and try to salvage some of our breakfast. It'll help clear my mind." I try to inject confidence in my tone. Having Willow out of the house is never easy for me but I don't want to take the risk of cancelling the whole visit if I go with her.

She pulls on her jacket and slides into her boots by the door. Willow blows me a kiss from across the room and I almost reach out to pretend I'm catching it. I wasn't even surprised by my re-action. Willow is disengaging my weapons and calling my soul back to her. The ice that has been surrounding me is melting in her constant presence.

This woman has me wrapped around her little finger and doesn't even know. I just have to hope she feels the same way. And it's been a really fucking long time since I hoped for anything at all.

twenty-five

willow

It totally floored me when Xander agreed to let Meredith come out here. I'm still trying to process this huge accomplishment for him, which is such an enormous step. Well, he needed some guidance and nudging but eventually Xander made a choice he should be proud of.

Dedication to this man flows through me like the blood in my veins. I want to be by his side always, through the good times and bad. I'll be here to experience every smile and laugh but also any struggle or argument that might come alone. No matter what, he's all mine.

My all-encompassing love for this stunning man amplifies further with each additional day. I want to bask in his profound shadow and continue soaking in his tantalizing company. Affection crashes over me and I find myself stunned that I lived so long without the knowledge of his true feelings. I need to open myself up completely and stop holding back.

I'm straight up giddy about the noticeable transformation with Xander. The strides he's made in such a short amount of time are really impressive. He's pushed through his panic like very few are able to do. Xander has given me everything I've asked for and exceeded any expectations I was stupid enough to set. He's inspired me and I'm ready to reveal all of my secrets. First we need to meet with his mother.

I spoke to Meredith about an hour ago and she was a blubbering mess once I told her the good news. She couldn't get out here fast enough, I guess, and even left her house while still talking to me on the phone. That warmed my heart. Xander was so loved but he wasn't at a point to accept that yet. He's getting closer each day though. This was proof of it.

Meredith should be here any moment and Xander's telltale signs of anxiety kick in with every second that passes. He was very specific in his demand to have her show up right away, which I totally understand. Once you've set your sights on something challenging, you want it over with quickly. Otherwise you start overthinking and creating mountains from anthills. I know this isn't easy for him and my concern increases with the severity of his agitated behavior.

The crunch of tires from outside alerts us of her arrival. Xander's erratic movements suddenly halt and his already tense body locks up further. I quickly move toward him and wrap my arm around his waist. I can feel his heart pounding through the connection. I slip my hand under his shirt so I get direct contact with his heated skin. As my fingers glide around his hip, Xander relaxes slightly.

I do my best to reassure him. "That's your mom out there, Xander. You know her better than anyone else. She is here because she loves you and wants to support you. Nothing will happen. If you want her to leave, just give me the signal and I'll tell her. I already talked to her about all of that and she totally understands. She's beyond excited just to see you. Even for a few minutes. All right?"

He doesn't say anything for a few beats and I'm worried Meredith won't get a glimpse of Xander before he pulls the plug. Then his rapid breathing begins to slow and he shakes out his rigid arms before seeking out my free hand. He grasps it tightly in his large palm and relaxes further.

When he speaks, his voice trembles slightly. "Don't let go, alright? I mean it. I can do this but I need you here. I don't care how that makes me sound. You're my strength when the darkness threatens to consume me. I'm really overwhelmed right now but I want this to happen. Can you open the door?"

This man continues to impress me. My brave friend. That title wasn't adequate anymore but hopefully we could figure that out after clearing this hurdle. I stand on my tiptoes to reach his mouth, which is as much for me as it is for him. Our lips meet for a brief kiss but so much power and strength passes between us for those short seconds.

Together we shuffle to the door before I unlock the series of deadbolts. I place my hand on the knob but look at Xander before twisting it. His eyes shine with bravery as his posture straightens with confidence. He clenches his jaw and a muscle tics in his cheek. Xander's face paints a complex canvas. So much is swirling within his blue depths but I'm pleased to see the most predominate is determination.

The deteriorating wood opens with a creak and a gust of freezing air greets us. Meredith is still sitting in her car but her gaze is intensely focused on our position. Tears are already streaming down her cheeks. My lips lift into an encouraging smile as I wave her way. Xander stands like stone at my side but at least he isn't retreating back into the house.

Meredith rushes out of her vehicle to greet us on the rickety porch. Her hurried steps cause her to stumble on the snowy terrain and I try to reach out with a helpful hand but am yanked back by Xander's unbreakable hold. When my confused gaze swings his way, I catch the distinct look of fear covering his entire face. Under his thatch of facial hair, his skin is ghostly white and drained of color. Xander's mouth is parted in shock and his expressive orbs are wide with dread.

I recognize that look immediately. More than ever, I will be his pillar to lean on. I squeeze his hand with mine for emphasis but I get no reaction.

Once his mom passes the slippery ground and rotting steps, she is standing a few feet from us. I used to see Meredith fairly often but it seems the last few months haven't been very kind to her. The usually perfect curls covering her head are flat and lifeless. Her makeup is smeared and a total wreck. The wrinkles she rightfully earned as a mother appear deeper than ever. I badly want to wrap my arms around her in a comforting embrace but I know Xander can't.

As if hearing my thoughts, Meredith shifts forward and reaches out to her son. That sudden movement wakes Xander from his paralyzed state and he staggers back on unsteady legs. Then something inside him snaps. It happened very suddenly but I swore I saw the shift happened in slow motion.

Xander was frightened and freaked out then his guard slammed down leaving him hollow and indifferent. I hadn't seen this side of him for several days and I wanted to stamp my foot in frustration. His top lip lifted into a snarl as he narrowed his eyes into furious slits. I have to turn this disaster around quickly. I refuse to watch him return to the empty shell he was hiding behind when I first arrived.

When my attention directs back to Meredith, I watch as her face crumples in agony. She dips her chin to hide the new onslaught of tears but her distress is displayed clearly enough across her defeated disposition for us to see. I tried to prepare Meredith when I spoke to her earlier but she's not handling this well. I'm not sure how much Xander is actually absorbing right now but hope he hasn't completely closed himself off.

My heart tears into two busted up pieces as these individuals suffer on separate sides. It's my job to bridge the freaking gap, which is going to require some serious intervention. My gaze swings between them a few times before I decide to break the silence.

"Alrighty! I think we need to start over. Xander?" I attempt to turn his mood around by gently stroking his arm. His head jerks, as though he's startled by touch, as his face tilts down toward me. Xander's stare is vacant but genuine warmth begins peeking through the gloom. A relieved sigh eases past my lips as I realize this isn't a lost cause.

Meredith is sniffling but otherwise remains quiet, which allows me to keep focusing on Xander. "Can you come back to me, please? You know I don't like it when you're grumpy." Our current situation is too serious so I try injecting a little sass.

Xander blinks slowly and his eyes gradually regain their usual dynamic layers. He leans closer until our foreheads touch. *"Willow."* His voice seems to rumble when he groans out my name. Xander's complexion was ashen as the agony continues to rush through him but at least he dodged the darkness.

My fingers edge along his jaw before cupping his cheek. "There you are. I see you, remember? I know you so well, Xander. Don't hide from me." I close my eyes as the words tumble out.

A choked gasp yanks us from our blissful bubble. I turn my head toward Meredith as she claps an open palm over her mouth. The tears are still flowing from her eyes but she looks . . . happy?

"I should go. You're dealing with too much already, Xander. I shouldn't have come. Not yet. Maybe we can talk soon, Willow? Take care of him for me, alright?" Meredith doesn't give me a chance to respond before she's turned around and racing to her car.

It can't end like this so I need to talk with her before she leaves. As if hearing my concern, Xander eases back to place a kiss on my temple before straightening to his full height. He's silently giving me permission to leave his side. He releases my hand from his grasp and I flash him a grateful smile before taking off down the wretched stairs.

Meredith is getting settled into her vehicle as I quickly arrive. "Wait! Please don't go." I skid to a stop near her open door and almost fall on my butt.

"Oh, sweetie. You don't need me here. I can see for myself that Xander is in very capable hands. I shouldn't have forced my way out here, especially not so soon. He isn't ready and I'm all right with that. The difference between now and when I last saw him is already significant. You've only been out here a few days. I am confident that you'll get our Xander back. An epiphany of sorts suddenly came to me, which had me realizing I need to leave. I'm fine, Willow. Don't you worry about me." Meredith is so calm all of a sudden and I don't quite understand the abrupt change. They didn't even talk.

"You can stay, Meredith. We can work something out. I didn't mean to make you feel unwelcome. Xander is dealing with a lot, yes, but he wanted to see you."

"Willow, don't start with that silly babble. You gave me the chance to see something truly special. What you two share is remarkable and it helps with my hurt knowing my son has you around. Keep doing what you're doing. How long can you stay out here with him?" Her question causes my chest to tighten. Thinking about leaving causes my pulse to skyrocket but it has to happen eventually.

I try to keep the wobble out of my tone. "I was able to get two weeks off work. I don't want to worry about that now though." My voice trails off as my gaze wanders to Xander.

"Do you really think we have a connection? You have no idea what that means to me, Meredith. You know how much I love Xander but I'm not sure how he feels. Spending all of this time alone with him has brought us close together but it could be due to convenience." My insecurities bleed out with that last statement.

Meredith scoffs while shaking her head. "That boy has always loved you, Willow. It's clearer now than ever. Before I go," she reaches into the backseat and produces a large duffel bag. "I brought you some clothes because your mother made it sound like you were in dire need. She packed the tote so don't get fussy with me. Now scoot and let me get out of here. You have your hands full." She shoos me away from her door but she isn't getting away that easily.

I clasp my arms around her shoulders and hug her like I wanted to earlier. "Thank you so much, Meredith. You have no idea what this means to me. I'm so thankful you made the trip out here, even though it didn't work out like we hoped. I'll call you soon, for sure. Drive safe." I murmur near her ear. She clutches me tight before pulling back. Meredith wipes below my eye and I realize I'm crying.

"We'll talk soon, Willow. Take care of each other. I'll tell your mother all is well." She winks and closes her door. Meredith starts her car, glances at Xander brooding on the porch, then drives away. I wave obnoxiously until my eyes lose sight of her.

When I turn back toward the house, Xander is still in the same spot. He looks pissed but that's pretty standard so I don't overthink it as I hoist my heavy bag over my shoulder. The closer I get, the more tension I feel radiating from his irritable form.

Once I'm standing before him, Xander says the last thing any woman wants to hear.

"We need to talk, Willow."

twenty-six

xander

I'm embarrassed as fuck that I had little control in stopping that bullshit from trying to take charge. I legit wanted to spend time with my mother, once I got over the initial shock. Clearly I wasn't ready for that, no matter how small the step appeared. I hope my mom can forgive me someday. I just can't worry about it right now.

Based off the enormous bag Willow is currently lugging up to the house, it's safe to assume she's sticking around for a bit. That soothes my jagged nerves but I'm still hesitant as fuck to confess the depth of my feelings for her. I'm done hiding that shit though. It's been eating at me for far too long.

The fucking black abyss almost swallowed me whole when my mother tried to touch me. I could sense the demons closing in and urging me to let them take over. The edges of my vision blurred and darkness started seeping in. I'd been so fucking close to the edge before Willow broke through. She saved me again. I'm beginning to lose track but it doesn't really matter. I owe her everything and I'm about to start paying her back.

My attention is hooked onto the woman swinging her hips my way as she struggles with her luggage. I need to take the plunge with Willow. She has always been the cure and she's the only one who can truly save me. I'm starting to think the truth will help set me free from the fucking clutches holding me captive to that horrific day and I am more than ready to be released from those fucking chains. I'm ready to let go of this shit once and for all.

When she finally reaches me on the landing, her effort puffs out in quickened breaths that are visible due to the chilled air. When I tell Willow we need to talk, I think she takes my message the wrong way based on her lack of eye contact and restless fidgeting. She doesn't respond either so that also alerts me to her unease. Does she really think I have anything bad to say? As if I'm going to tell her to hit the road and never come back. That's a fucking joke.

I snatch the bag from her arm, something I should have done right away, before following her into the house. I'll end this misery soon enough and hopefully bring the light back to her beautiful eyes.

Once I've closed and secured the busted door, I turn to find Willow facing the bay window I recently uncovered. The view into the forest is something that shouldn't be kept hidden and I was an idiot to boarding it up in the first place. When she suggested tearing down the barricades, I couldn't agree fast enough. The grin that overtook her face was worth every splinter I received while ripping the wood down.

The sun shining through the unobstructed glass causes Willow to glow, which is extremely fitting. This woman is my angel. I stroll up behind her and place my hands on her hips. She tries to turn around so she can look at me but I hold her in place. I won't be able to admit everything if Willow is staring directly at me and imploring me with all-knowing eyes.

My throat is tight with the words I've kept buried and held hostage for too long, before stalling on my tongue.

I need to stop being such a fucking pansy.

I lower my head until my chin rests on her shoulder and try to steady my voice as I unleash my secrets. She presses her forehead against mine and I don't stop her movement this time. The intimate connection makes this moment even more powerful.

"More than ever I wish I was better at expressing my feelings, but I'll do my best to explain. It's your turn to listen, all right?" I wait for her to acknowledge my request. When she nods, I start down the path that will undoubtedly alter our relationship but could lead to our future.

"I'm in love with you, Willow." I don't let the sharp hitch in her breath deter me. "The deep, life changing, irrecoverable, all consuming kind. I have been since the moment I first met you, which was well before I actually understood the weight of the concept. You mean everything to me. You're so fucking vital that it's difficult to breathe when you're not around. I didn't always understand these feelings but they've always been there. Burning inside of me and growing stronger each time I saw your beautiful face." I inhale her lavender scent before slowly exhaling to continue.

"You're my best friend but I've always wanted more than that. Before I enlisted, it never felt like the right time to cross the line with you. I was just a punk kid with nothing to offer. *Fuck*, how much time we've wasted. I want nothing more than to go back to those early years and slap some sense into myself.

"I want to protect you, Willow. *Possess you.* Share my life with you as we grow old together. Always be blessed with your blinding presence." I end my procession with a delicate kiss on her neck.

She shivers slightly before settling her head back against my chest. Her eyes are closed but I notice the tracks of tears on her rosy cheeks.

Shit, why is she crying?

Willow sniffles before clearing her throat. If I were a betting man, I'd go all in on this ending badly. If I were a religious man, I'd send a prayer up to the heavens for my case.

"Tell me what you're thinking, Willow."

Her watery eyes blink open and I'm immediately lost within their emerald depths. "Oh my gosh, Xander. Seriously, wow." She chuckles at her bumbling.

Her next words are barely audible but I feel them deep within my soul. "I'm so in love with you. I've been waiting so long to hear you say those words. I'm a little unbalanced because I'm trying to absorb the fact you love me too. I've dreamed of this moment since I was a little girl." Her gorgeous lips tip up into a stunning smile, showcasing her happiness. I can't resist kissing her there as well.

She loves me.

The girl I've always been crazy about just mirrored my infatuation. I can't fucking believe this is happening. What did I do to deserve the devotion of this woman? I'm not going to waste time questioning it.

"There's not a single doubt about how I feel. I want it all with you, Willow. Let me show you how much I care about you. Let my body communicate the admission I can't properly describe." I utter my desire and her tongue peeks out of her succulent mouth. I almost groan at the invitation to devour her.

I'm glad we're on the same page.

When she whispers, "Make me yours, Xander," I just about bust in my pants.

As if I need further encouragement, Willow plants her palms on my thighs and glides them up to my groin. My hips involuntarily rock forward into her ass. There is no denying the physical reaction she evokes in me so I want to drive her equally wild with want. When I get between her legs, she better be soaked with desire and incoherent with need.

This is going to be a long fucking night.

My arms loop around her waist so I can whip her shirt off. Once the top is out of my way, I stroke the expanse of her freshly exposed skin. My rough fingers on her silky flesh makes a tantalizing contrast.

Before I get too carried away, I need to give Willow something very special to me. There is another token that proves how serious I am about her. I dig the dog tags out of my pocket and slip the cool metal over her head. She releases a startled gasp at the cold sensation against her heated skin.

I give her more of the sweet stuff. "My heart is yours and I want you to always keep me close. These belong to you, just like I do." I give the strand a gentle tug for emphasis before continuing.

"In the military, these are the most important form of identification for a soldier. Now they symbolize that you're a part of me." With those words from me, Willow grasps the tags in her hand before lifting them to her mouth.

When she places a delicate kiss along the engraving, I forget everything else besides showering this woman with my undying love. I resume my physical seduction to her body by swiping my palms along her tits and pinching her hardened nipples. Willow is already getting desperate with longing as her enticing form wriggles against me, begging and urging me on.

I spin her around to face me before easily lifting her to straddle my hips. Once my hands are firmly placed under her ass and her ankles cross behind my back, I stride to the bed. Willow begins to suck on my neck, which causes my feet to slide along the wooden floor in my haste. My demand for her is igniting an unstoppable flame that is threatening to combust. I imagine the heat will soon take over both of us. I can almost taste the lust crawling up my limbs.

As if sensing the proximity to our desired location, Willow loosens her death grip. I toss her down onto the center of the bed and she scoots further up toward the headboard.

Her dark hair fans out on the white pillow like a dirty halo but there is nothing filthy about her. Everything about my girl is pure and good, which is part of the reason I'm so fucking mesmerized.

I stand at the edge of the mattress and take a moment to appreciate her natural beauty. Her green eyes are lit with hunger and her cheeks are flushed with arousal. Willow arches her back, which pushes her ample tits higher in the air. The sight of my tags hanging between her breasts really turns me on. Everyone will know who she belongs to, which has my cock harder than a lead pipe.

Her breathing is rushing out in uneven pants as she continues to get worked up. One of her hands glides along her exposed nipples while the other begins to travel lower. Her toned stomach flexes with her movements and I want to lick a path down the middle until I hit her heated core. Her narrow hips are shifting restlessly and I can tell she won't wait for me much longer.

Just as that thought passes through my mind, Willow reaches for me while humming another, *"Please."* Who am I to deny her?

With fake calmness, I prowl forward and cover her body with mine. Her eager hands glide up my arms until they reach my shoulders. I dip my mouth to hers and suck on her lower lip before diving my tongue inside. Willow immediately matches my aggressive strokes with her own, earning a low moan from me. Her soothing touch seeps down into my bones, which engulfs my entire being in scorching heat.

I swivel my pelvis into her lower half, making sure Willow feels how stiff she's making me.

Fuck, I don't think I can wait much longer.

Breaking away from her mouth is a challenge but I'm desperate to taste more of her sweetness. It's all teeth, lips, and tongue as I move from her neck to her glorious tits.

The luscious mounds make me fucking starving so I quickly work on devouring them. Willow's nipples are hard peaks that I eagerly suck deep into my mouth. She claws at my scalp and goes nutty due to my actions. I'm going to mark her again, which might be savage as hell, but I could give a fuck. While my mouth is latched onto her breasts, my hand snakes down her delectable waist between us. I work my palm under the elastic of her pants in order to reach her bare pussy. Just as I hoped, Willow is fucking slick with desire. Her essence coating my fingers is such a huge turn on that I feel my dick get impossibly harder. I need to taste her sweetness then bury myself deep inside her.

I release the suction on her nipple before dragging my tongue down her belly. I sit up on my knees so I can pull Willow's leggings off. My greedy mouth follows the trail of fabric and her creamy flesh instantly has an uncontainable craving pooling in my throat. She's damn delicious so I nip and lick along her legs until Willow's impatient whines bring me back to her center.

Once she's completely naked and spread out before me, I thank my lucky fucking stars that this extraordinary beauty loves me. She's the most gorgeous woman I've ever seen, inside and out. Right now though, I'm focusing on the dripping spot between her thighs.

Sexy as fuck.

I don't waste any more time getting my mouth on her velvet core. Her fingers resume clutching at my hair as she allows me to take control of her body. Once my lips make contact, Willow melts and opens under me. As though she's never wanted anything as badly as this. Her whimpers and moans morph into pleas, which exponentially escalates my appetite and I'm fucking starving. I can't tease her much longer.

I scrape my flattened tongue down her slit and back up through her delicious seam. I stop for a moment to inhale her musky scent and bury my nose in her honey. She releases her fistfuls of my hair in order to glide her palms down to my shoulders. The gentle slide of her smooth skin against me has an involuntary shudder rolling through me. The sensation encourages me to work even harder to ensure Willow is consumed with the same pleasure as me.

Her swollen clit is begging for attention that I'm happy to give. The bundle is easy to find and is peeking out for me to see. I lap at the little nerve button and Willow shudders in response. I swear more delectable nectar flows out and I eagerly quench my thirst by drinking her up.

When I add a finger into the mix, Willow squeals and starts thrashing her head against the pillow. Her nails will surely leave scratches on my skin as they dig into me deeper and I'm not shocked at how much the thought excites me. Once I sink another digit into her quivering tightness, Willow begins bucking her hips, so I cinch an arm around her pelvis to hold her in place. Then I really get into it.

My tongue is working relentless circles around her clit while I work my fingers steadily into her slick core. I reach to hit the spot that I know sets Willow off and once I get there, her body erupts in uncontrollable trembles. Her grip on me is painful, but feels so fucking good, I might come in my briefs.

The sounds coming out of her mouth are nonsense but make me think I've pushed Willow past the edge of sanity. Her release is pouring out of her and I can't swallow fast enough. I could eat Willow for all three meals and be completely fucking satisfied. I want to feast on her all night but if I don't get some relief, my cock will burst.

I'm still licking up her juices and giving gentle strokes with my finger when Willow eases down from her epic orgasm. She loosens her death grip on my scalp in order to grab my shoulders and encourage me up her body. I'm just as fucking eager but the whisker burn on Willow's inner thighs catches my attention. The skin is irritated and red because of what I just did to her. The sight is a fantasy come to life and I have to clench my eyes shut to avoid embarrassing myself. I'm damn fucking proud of leaving evidence of where I've been and I hope she will appreciate my brand all over her.

I place a light kiss along the trail before raising my head to catch her stare. Willow's eyes are glazed over and reflecting so much passion.

This woman effortlessly pushes me past any boundary I ever had and I fucking love it. I can't keep the growl out of my voice when I say, "I see you, Willow. You're so fucking gorgeous all crazed and gasping. Are you ready to be completely mine?"

twenty-seven

willow

E*ff me.*

What the actual heck was that? Xander has been holding out on me. Him going down on me was freaking mind blowing.

My lady bits are still trying to recover and Xander is tossing that sexy line my way that obliterate any progress in the recuperation department. As if he actually has to ask if I want to be his. I start nodding frantically and I can't agree fast enough. I'm eager to have his full weight blanketing me as I accept him into my body.

Gosh, he's so freaking sinful.

His beard is wet from me and that shouldn't turn me on, but it has my pussy purring in delight. The fact he got me so drenched that I've covered him is pretty impressive.

Now he's licking his plump lips and moaning at what he finds there.

Why do I find that so hot? Cheese and rice, he's turning me into a sex addict.

Xander slithers along my body and each place he touches erupts in flames. The reactions this guy evokes within me are so intense. My clit is still vibrating with tiny shocks ricocheting about. It's never, ever been like this for me before. I had no idea sex could be so rewarding.

I open my legs wider to accommodate his huge form before he settles between them. My muscles stretch to bracket him and the burn is yummy. Xander props up on his left elbow to keep some weight off me but I'm desperate for it all. My arms loop around his middle to yank him down but he doesn't budge.

Darn.

Xander takes his free hand and swipes some errant strands of hair from my forehead. He leans down to place a barely there kiss on my temple and my insides turn mushy. This sweet side of him is turning me into a gooey mess. His nose brushes along my jaw until he reaches my ear. Then he murmurs, "I love you", before pulling back to catch my gaze.

The smile taking over my face probably looks ridiculous but I don't mind. I want Xander to know every piece of me.

"I love you too, X. So very much." I give him the last part I was holding back. Moisture gathers in my eyes so I blink quickly to clear it. I cup his scruffy cheek and don't miss the shock as it passes through his expressive ocean eyes. When I notice them getting misty, the lump in my throat grows larger.

Xander glances away briefly to collect himself before responding. "I didn't realize I needed to hear that so much or how much I missed you calling me that." He gives his head a little shake before inching closer to almost touch my lips with his.

"Wills," he breathes into my gasping mouth. I shudder at the name I haven't heard in three long years. I want him inside me so badly it burns.

I arch my back as he shifts lower, which causes his solid shaft to grind against me in the most delicious way. "Oh my goodness, that's feels so freaking amazing!" I yelp out when his dick rubs against an especially sensitive spot perfectly. I lose all train of thought and focus only on what Xander is doing.

I moan before Xander's hungry mouth descends upon mine. This kiss starts out different from anything we've previously shared. We take our time to explore and enjoy. The affection pours out between us and releases a flurry of pent up emotions. Our lips effortlessly slip together to create a tight seal that is freaking magical. Our tongues begin a slow erotic dance while our heads tilt to get impossibly closer. Xander's palm is holding my jaw and my fingers spear into his untamed hair. Our lower halves are rocking together and I'm so freaking wet that Xander's hardness easily strokes through my crease. I could definitely get off from this alone.

All of a sudden it changes, like we snap and cannot hold back our driving need any longer. Our kiss becomes sloppy and messy, like we are purposely missing the target or coloring outside the lines. Our touches spread farther and become more aggressive. One of my hands is clutching Xander's thrusting bum and the other is clasped around his Willow tattoo. His palm drags down my body, which awakens every tiny nerve ending. He finds my tingling clit smashed between us, which makes me jolt from Xander's lips so I can yell out in pleasure.

Holy crap, this man has mad skills.

Xander sucks a line from my chin to my neck before licking his way to my breasts. Once he latches onto my nipple, the desperation to have him deep inside takes over my entire being.

"Please, X . . . I need you. Don't make me wait again. Make love to me." I'm whining and moaning but I could care less. This man is breaking me apart with his seductive movements.

Once my plea registers, Xander shifts slightly and I can feel him *right there*. One thrust and he will ease this aching emptiness. Before I can ask again, he plunges into me with his massive cock.

Oh. My. Gawd!

My mouth drops open in a soundless scream. My inner walls strain with the enormous intrusion but the breach feels fantastic. Xander slides deep and hits a particular place that has my limbs spasming with convulsions. I whimper and dig my nails deeper into his butt, urging him on. I alternate my begging between *again, more, yes*, and *please*.

Together we are jolts of friction, sparking anywhere we touch. Our hips are magnetic. The coarse hair on his legs is abrasive against the smooth skin of mine. Our chests are bumping and rubbing with vigor. The sound of sliding skin is music to my freaking ears. The longer Xander pounds into me, the higher I soar. Electricity is pulsing/surging through my veins and I've never felt better.

No words are needed. Everything we need to say is expressed through our flesh. Each soft caress. Every gentle glide of fingers. Delicate kisses with heavy meaning. Our bodies are having a conversation far deeper than any verbal exchange could name. I feel like Xander is reciting a poem to my soul with every drive into my core. What is happening feels meant to be on an instinctual level. Even if we tried to stop, the force binding us together is too strong.

My heart and mind are yearning for this joining right along with my body. I trace the thick veins on his sinewy forearms, which cranks my arousal up another notch. I had no idea I could ever feel something like this. The pleasure is so extreme. Xander yanks me from my mental trance when he purrs straight sexiness in my ear.

"You're so damn tight, Willow. I can't remember anything ever being this good. I want this to last so I can savor and cherish you but I don't think I can handle it. Your pussy is squeezing my dick so fucking hard." His powerful pumps seem perfectly coordinated with his words.

For a man that claims he doesn't use words well, he sure knows his way around dirty talk. I'm freaking loving this side of Xander.

He keeps going since I'm apparently stunned silent. "You're soaking. Do you like this? Am I making you feel good?" I can only answer in breathy moans and panting gasps as Xander completely dominates me.

He props up on an elbow in order to look down to where we are intimately and erotically connected. Xander bites his bottom lip and moans at the sight. He slips his fingers around the root of his cock so he can feel the penetration. It makes me freaking crazed and gives another layer of fantastic friction.

When he pushes in, I tilt my pelvis up to accept him even deeper. When he pulls back, I grip his butt and clasp my legs tighter to stop him from retreating too far. I can feel his cock growing impossibly thicker inside of me. The added pressure causes my internal muscles to clench and contract. Every long, torturous drag is delicious.

I'm feeling desperate for release so I push myself to speak. I'm not above begging. "Xander, I need to come. *Please.* I want it so bad." I end my frazzled rant on a sigh.

"Give in to me, Wills." He whispers near my ear before gently biting the lobe. Then he strums my clit with his thumb and after only a few swipes, the fierce orgasm smashes through me.

I'm shaking uncontrollably as heat engulfs my entire body. The spasms begin at my core but rapidly flow outward to conquer me completely. My body is taken over by convulsions that keep expanding and extending until I'm no longer in charge of my actions.

What is happening to me?

As my release is blasting through me, I barely register

Xander's thrusts becoming more frenzied and punishing. I'm gasping for air and trying to stay conscious through this intoxication. His jaw clamps down on my shoulder as my nails brutally dig into his skin.

"Fuck. *Fuck!* I'm going to come, Willow. I need to pull out." Xander sounds savage as he begins jerking above me.

I lock my ankles around his hips while screaming, "Don't you freaking dare."

Once the words leave my mouth, Xander slams into me a final time and reaches a spot that's never been touched before. His corded body bows and writhes as he empties everything he's got inside my dripping core. His groan is guttural and the sound sets off another round of violent shudders within me.

When the twitching and tingling eventually subsides, I feel Xander bite down on my sensitive flesh before his face settles in the crook of my neck.

I shiver when his heated breath skates across my sweaty skin. "I can't deny that I love my marks covering you and knowing your pussy is flooded with my cum. I don't give a shit if that makes me barbaric. I've claimed you and now you're mine. You've always been mine, Wills." His voice is so raw and untamed, matching his words perfectly.

Well, stick a fork in me because I am freaking done.

———◆———

THE EUPHORIA CONTINUES buzzing through my blood while we lounge in bed awhile later. I'm still processing Xander's declaration of love and the fact he's been hiding these feelings since we were kids. It totally boggles my mind that we kept this huge secret from one another. I would like to assume life would have been far smoother if we took the plunge way back then by confessing our truths. I release a hefty exhale and Xander tightens his arm around me.

The fact we are cuddling right now is exciting enough. I absolutely enjoy the physical aspects, especially what we've shared, but lying here in compassionate silence is just as amazing. Xander is leisurely running his fingers through my hair while I lazily pet his chiseled chest. The blissful state we're in causes our relaxed breathing to sync as the air easily escapes our lips. I'm so freaking happy and I feel like I'm floating.

Before finding Xander again, I almost gave up hope that us being together, like this, was ever going to happen. I'm so thankful for that surviving sliver I managed to hold onto. I could never let Xander go completely, so my heart hums happily since my optimism has been justified. I snuggle deeper into his embrace as I count my numerous blessings.

I'm content and comfortable as I gaze up at Xander's handsome face. He notices me looking and brushes a soft kiss on my forehead. I sleepily sigh, "I love you, X." The words fall from my lips without warning but it makes sense for the moment.

Xander's body goes rigid and his hand freezes against my scalp. He clears his throat. "I'm still not used to hearing you say that. It's difficult for me to believe you could possibly feel that way for me, especially after everything I've put you through. You deserve so much better than a broken man like me but I'll never take your love for granted." His mouth is against my temple and his warm breath sends shivers across my chilled skin. I hate the defeated tone of his voice but he continues before I can comment on it.

"I love you so fucking much, Wills. I'll spend the rest of my years proving that to you. Life has been so fucking dark, but since you've been around, there is blinding light reflecting everywhere." His hushed statements cause my heart to take off in rapid beats. It feels like it could burst out of my chest.

I feel pressure behind my eyes as tears begin forming. I lower my lashes to hide the emotion but Xander grasps my chin to tilt my head up. He moves impossibly closer before banding his arms more securely around my waist. I feel protected and taken care of when pulled so close to him that I'm not surprised to feel the first drop trail down my cheek. I release a small chuckle at my reaction but suck in a gasp when Xander licks the tear away.

"I see you, Wills. Don't hide from me, baby. Never keep anything from me ever again." He places a devastating kiss along my lips that has my wild imagination spinning up a romantic fairytale where we live happily ever after. A swarm of butterflies erupt in my belly at his continued display of tenderness.

Being with Xander is second nature. It comes easy, like we just click. Once we got past that initial awkward stage, we effortlessly picked up where we left off. As though nothing had changed and time hadn't been ripped away from us.

I want this to work out so badly my soul vibrates with need. I love this man with my entire being but I'm terrified it will slip from my grasp. I wish we could remain hidden out here in the woods forever but that's not realistic for either of us. This is not the time to start obsessing over potential threats to our relationship. We are here now, together, where I've dreamed of being for so long.

When he breaks the kiss, the look of love shining from his eyes causes another lump to form in my throat.

"These past three years I was alive but I wasn't living, Willow. I was barely scraping by, stuck in a never-ending nightmare. The darkness consumed me and my reality was bleak as fuck. I didn't believe I'd survive, and to be honest, most days I didn't want to. Now though, you've given me a reason to live again."

With those words, he's totally destroyed me. I'm ruined in the most exquisite way. I'm all freaking choked up so I show him what I can't currently explain. I roll him onto his back before straddling his hips. I lean down to capture his mouth in a searing kiss as I glide my pussy along his hardening shaft. It doesn't take long for him to be ready and I lift up to welcome him into my depths.

We continue whispering our confessions and truths as we join together. Our secrets spill out into the dark room.

This time we go slow and sweet, all night long.

twenty-eight

willow

I wake up from the sun streaking through the window and flooding the room with bright light. I'm sprawled across Xander and I've never slept better. My subtle movements alert Xander of my rousing and he squeezes my butt before grinding his morning wood into my tired pussy. She needs a serious time out.

"Good morning," he grumbles in a drowsy tone.

Mmmm, good morning indeed.

I shift my pelvis away from his massive erection to dissuade him from getting any ideas. Xander huffs out a breath in fake annoyance before smacking my retreating bum. I yelp and glare up into his smiling eyes. It's difficult to tell if his lips are tipped up with all that facial hair obstructing the view.

A question that's been bouncing around randomly pops into my brain. I worry about disrupting our playful mood but my curiosity wins out.

"Can I ask you something?" I begin after clearing my dry throat. Xander freezes slightly beneath me but nods in approval.

"I've been super curious about your beard ever since I saw you again. Growing up, you were always clean cut so it got me wondering. Don't get me wrong, you look really hot, but is there a reason for it?" I ask while resting my chin on his chest. My head rides his deep inhale and drops back down when he releases it.

Xander's gaze darts away nervously before refocusing on me. "Well, it's kind of a long story and definitely not amusing or interesting, so don't get your hopes up." He appears worried and edgy, which has my mind reeling with possibilities. His audible sigh accompanies his discomfort as he scratches his fuzzy neck.

"The beard started as a cover to hide a hideous scar running along my cheek and jaw." As Xander speaks, he grabs my right hand and presses it against his face. He gently glides my fingertips along a bumpy ridge that isn't visible but is noticeable through touch. The wound must have been enormous because the jagged line is really thick and long. I rub along the edges while combing through his beard and try to imagine what could have caused such an injury.

I don't want to force details from him but Xander has to know I'm curious to hear much more about this topic. Laying my ear against his pec allows me to hear his steady heartbeat while my eyes search deep into his with an unwavering stare.

Xander makes a choking sound that could almost pass for a chuckle. "Damn, you're so fucking cute. Tell me what you want to know, Willow." His expression is open and willing so I take advantage.

"Will you tell me how it happened? I'm assuming it goes along with why you've locked yourself away out here. That's a huge scar so it can't be from tripping down those nasty stairs outside." The corner of my lip tips up at my attempt to inject some humor but I know this is a pivotal moment for us.

He expels another weighty gust of air that wafts across my face. "This shit is impossible to even think about. I've never talked to anyone about what happened that day. Plenty tried, especially when I was in the hospital. This story is pitch black and I don't want to dim your light. It's so fucking vicious and dirty." Xander's voice is trembling, which causes my throat to tighten with guilt for putting him in this position. Before I can protest, he keeps going.

"I hate imagining it but I'll tell you everything, if you want to listen. If it helps you feel closer to me, I'll let it all out." He wheezes out the words while tightening his grip on my waist.

I take a few seconds to collect myself and determine how to respond. Everyone handles grief differently but Xander has been storing so much pain without an outlet. Anyone can see he's not been properly managing whatever is bottled up in his beautiful brain.

With those driving thoughts as motivation, I strengthen my resolve and decide I want him to release his demons. No matter what.

"Since you've been gone, I've constantly wondered what took you away from me. I'm desperate to find out, but I want you to do it for you, not for me. Let it out for you, Xander." Moisture blurs my vision so I wipe my lids before it gets worse.

"This is for us, Wills. So we can move forward. *Together.* I can't get this shit off my chest without you beside me, all right? You've already helped me by making all this shit seem better. It will feel good to share it with you." Xander's tone is so sincere and kind that the tears collect faster than I can stop them. The emotion is spilling across my cheeks but he swipes the drops away with his thumb.

A hollow laugh escapes my throat. "You haven't told me anything and I'm already a freaking mess. Gosh." I blink quickly a few times in an attempt to stem the flow. My watery eyes look up and get caught up in his calm blue ones. The cleansing breath

I release brings clarity to my mind.

"I will carry this burden with you. I would do anything for you, X." I feel like I'm whispering those truths directly into his soul.

A single tear trickles down his cheek and it nearly breaks me. Xander nods his head once before speaking. "All right. Well, I've already told you a little bit about the men that I served with. Over the two years I was actively deployed overseas, we were all stationed together in several cities throughout Afghanistan. Since our troop consisted of only ten soldiers, we became really close without much effort. They were my brothers. Men I would gladly have standing next to me on my wedding day. Paul Collins was my best friend over there and it guts me daily that I'll never fucking see his face again." His body is shaking slightly against mine and I can almost hear his heart pounding an anxious rhythm. I bite my lip in worry that these recollections are already taking a toll. I hug my arms around his middle in a silent show of support.

After a few moments, Xander picks up where he left off. "Over there, in the middle of the fucking desert, your reality is warped. It is a completely different dynamic and it's tough to explain. You bond through experience and quickly learn to rely on them. After several months of dull repetition in horrible conditions, the mood around camp was pretty giddy because new orders came through that we were getting pulled out in a few weeks. Of course, there would be several stops in between. Depending on your situation, you either head home or ship out to the next mission. I hadn't signed my reenlist papers. By that point, I was ready to come home to you." About halfway through, Xander tips his head to the side so he can be closer to me. I close the gap by leaning up to place a delicate kiss on his lips. This man is ripping me apart and I freaking love it.

I pull back after a few beats so we won't get too off track. The affection shining from his glossy irises makes me swoon. I bring my palm up to cup Xander's scruffy jaw before running my fingers through his coarse beard. He moans in pleasure and the noise almost has me rethinking the direction our morning is headed. I scratched my nails along his skin a few more times before tucking my hand under his shoulder again.

Xander understands that's his cue to continue. "This is where shit gets fucked up. Bear with me during this part, yeah?"

I'm nodding before he finishes the question.

"Our typical day involved routine checks and general maintenance of the surrounding area. We were often on patrols together, which was great because no one got left behind. The town we were stationed in was a non-hostile area so there shouldn't have been a risk. We were fortunate to be away from active fighting and combat zones. We passed through that small community several times a week to meet with our civilian allies. They were our ears and eyes on the streets, just in case a gang got ballsy and tried to riot. We were just there to ensure the peace was being kept, which pissed off a lot of locals. By this time, most of the serious fighting was over but sometimes a rebel group would strike.

"On this particular day, it was my turn to talk with our sources. Everyone else planned to move forward and I'd meet them at the checkpoint a block away. As soon as I got out of the truck, I had a funny feeling. People always say that when something horrible is about to happen but for me it was true. This fucking gut instinct. There was no indication or intel of a threat at our usual stop so I went along with protocol. I'd completed the same damn recon countless times so I shook off the bullshit feeling.

"That was the biggest mistake of my life. We never saw it coming, Willow. One minute, my brothers were alive and fucking well. Collins was smiling at me while telling me to hurry up, which was so fucking typical. They were all joking around and being a bunch of idiots. I remember laughing with them and thinking life ain't too bad.

"The next, there was a catastrophic blast that rocked the fucking ground I'd been standing on. I had just started moving toward the building when the Humvee soared through the air like a fucking rocket. My buddies were screaming, bleeding out, *and fucking dying*, while I lay in the fucking dirt unable to move. I was in and out of consciousness but I tried so fucking hard to reach them. My brothers were taking their last breaths and I didn't do a damn thing to help them.

"I have no clue how long I was trapped in that somewhat lucid state but it couldn't have been long. Soon enough shit went black and the next time I woke up, I was in the fucking hospital with no memories. *Zero.* I was stuck in this fucking limbo because I couldn't recall a damn thing. I was surrounded by strangers that didn't fucking understand what the hell was wrong with me.

"My physical injuries were really significant so I couldn't fucking move. I was stuck in a bed for weeks before they let me up on my own. Even then, I was under constant surveillance. Apparently, I was a serious flight risk and a threat to myself, like a fucking loon." Xander was spitting the words like venom. I rubbed along his scalp in an attempt to soothe him.

After taking a few deep breaths, he kept going. "I'm still bitter about all that medical bullshit. I spent months balancing on the edge of sanity while trying to recall anything from my life before I became a blank slate. It was torture, Willow. I didn't think it could get much worse, until one random day, the visions began swooping in. The images were exact replicas of that day, over and over. Similar to echoes but out of fucking nowhere. Once that started, I was begging for the ignorant numbness to return. I couldn't fucking concentrate without hearing voices. If someone touched me, I went berserk. The doctors tried to talk to me, but I wasn't fucking interested in their bullshit. The hallucinations haunted me constantly and slowly started driving me crazy. It was fucking hell and I couldn't stand it." Xander's tone is coated with so much disdain that a shudder rolls through me.

With a grunt, Xander continues. "Eventually I was able to create a version of normal that the doctors and authorities accepted. It was fucking bogus since I was wracked with nightmares nonstop. I couldn't handle being stuck in that place another day though and I was desperate. I was transferred to a military base in Maryland for additional debriefing and mandatory therapy. More intensive shit that I didn't want to deal with but faked my way through it. After several weeks, I was finally given the all clear and honorably discharged. They thanked me for my service and explained how vital my time in the army was. It didn't feel like the right thing but I took off without a backward glance." Xander growls as his teeth grind down hard. He yanks at his hair while clenching his jaw before he's ready to tell me the rest. My heart and mind are sobbing in sorrow for him. I clutch one of his tight fists with my hands before bring it to my lips for a soft kiss. I can only hope he hears my silent support.

"I hitched any ride I could find to reach Minnesota. I didn't have a plan other than getting the fuck away from society. I stumbled on this cabin by accident and the owner was more than willing to rent it out. Pretty positive no one has lived here in years but I didn't require anything fancy. I moved in almost two months ago, right around the year anniversary of the ambush. I was really fucking glad to be alone but I almost didn't survive that night."

"Since then, I've kept to myself out here. I was plagued with thoughts of my fallen brothers and how I should have died with them. They were my fucking team and I deserted them by staying alive. I didn't feel deserving of life so I caved to the constant destruction and debilitation my mind put me through. Just what I thought I wanted, until you showed up." He clears his throat nervously before shifting his gaze from the ceiling to my face.

His eyes scour into my soul as he waits for my reaction but I need a quick minute to compose myself. I am stunned speechless after everything he just revealed. Xander has openly communicated with me about the worst year of his life and I'm freaking gutted with misery. I'm overcome by gut-wrenching agony as I envision everything the love of my life went through. Everything in my body pangs with deep-seated hurt as though I'm physically wounded by his story. I had no clue about the heavy weight of grief he has been dragging around for so long or the daily battles Xander fights with his mind.

This is beyond belief and once again I find myself wishing I could have been with him through all of this. My soul was slashed with how distant we'd become and I found myself frequently calling out to Xander in my dreams. Maybe this was a huge part of that. Secretly I knew he was suffering and I should have been by his side. I'm so freaking thankful that we are together through this now.

He should have been done with combat after leaving the military but he was still waging war daily. I feel so grateful that he chose me.

My heart bleeds for this man, my sweet friend and passionate lover. I cried the entire time Xander was talking but thankfully it didn't seem to distract him. He survived such a horrific incident and he hates himself for it. To be the only remaining individual from such a tight knit group would be devastating.

Xander has so much contempt for himself and actually thinks he should have died too. My soul is weeping for it's other half, which makes my chest feel like caving in. My eyes burn and my head is spinning. I'm worn out from slamming through a spectrum of emotions. I try to collect my thoughts and formulate words so I can give Xander the response he deserves.

"I can't tell you enough how proud I am of you, Xander. Not only for what you accomplished during your time in the service, but more importantly for coming back alive. If you weren't here right now, I wouldn't have you in my arms. We would have never confessed the love between us. I would have lived my life without you and that would've slowly continued to break me. You have brought true happiness back into my bland existence and for that, I am so blessed. We have each other again, Xander. Thank you for making your way back to me." I almost don't finish my declaration before the emotion takes over.

Tears slide down my heated cheeks but I'm beyond the point of caring. This man has given me everything so I won't hide from him. Xander swipes a few errant streaks away before placing a gentle peck on my pouty mouth. He hums deep in his throat, which says so much without uttering a syllable. When he leans back, I'm shocked for an entire different reason.

A genuine smile is cracking his stony exterior and lifting his usually flat lips. Xander's grim demeanor vanishes with this display of joy. My breath hitches and fire floods my veins as I continue soaking this rarity in.

Don't get me wrong, Xander has always been an extremely attractive male specimen, but his surly attitude could be slightly off-putting when he never flashed a grin. The sullen Grizzly Adams look really works for him though and adds to his overall appeal. Throwing this smirk into the mix is totally lethal and potent. I don't stand a freaking chance. My mouth hangs open in shock as my cheeks heat to a furious degree. He must find my stunned stupor hilarious because he actually releases a hint of a laugh. That tiny chuckle is catastrophic to my lady bits and does funny things to my heart. As if the smile wasn't sexy enough.

Cheese and rice.

Xander doesn't spend much time focusing on my reaction before circling back to the original topic. "So, the beard started as camouflage but morphed into laziness. I didn't care that I was still breathing, much less what I looked like. Maybe now is the time for a shave. What do you think? Will you help me, Wills?" The delight shining from his eyes is dazzling.

"Abso-freaking-lutely. Especially if you keep smiling. Where are the hedge clippers?"

He snorts at my choice of words and giddy butterflies erupt in my belly. I realize my Xander has been here the entire time, I've just finally rediscovered him.

twenty-nine

xander

O nce I purged all the details of the ambush, it felt like a
heavy load had been lifted from my chest. Willow and
I seem even closer, which I didn't think was possible.
The way she is looking at me, with so much love and faith, has
my heart soaring and my cock hardening. What can I say? I'm still
a fucking man. One who happens to be totally pussy whipped.
When she was nestled between my legs to help me shave, it tested
every last bit of my wavering control.

My mind is quietly peaceful when she stares at me like I'm
her reason for living. This sense of calm hasn't resonated within
me since I left for boot camp.

That thought has a memory floating down on me.

*Willow was at my house and we were watching some comedy she
picked out. We were sitting way too close on the couch to be considered
friendly, but that's how we were. Willow's head was perched on my*

shoulder while she skated her fingers along my forearm. She had her legs draped over my lap so my palm rested on her thigh.

I was tenting some serious wood but that was nothing new. I had a perpetual hard on for this girl and my balls had a serious case of the blues.

Willow was all I could think about but I made a pretty huge choice today, so I wasn't able to focus on the movie for shit. A chill covered my skin when I thought of how Willow would react when I told her I'd finally decided to enlist in the military. I internally smacked myself for this wishy-washy nonsense. I cleared my throat and prepare to just blurt it out.

"Hey Wills? I wanna tell you something. Don't freak out, all right?" She lifted her head so she could look at my face before lifting an inquisitive eyebrow. That was her confirmation to continue.

"I spoke to a recruiter for the Army today. Remember I mentioned I was considering it? Well, I'm going to join once I'm eighteen. He assured me I would remain stateside for a large portion of my contract but there's a chance I'll go overseas." Pretty sure that all came out in one breath because my lungs were burning once I finished.

I heard Willow suck in a gasp halfway through my speech so I wasn't surprised to see the concerned expression on her face. I squeezed her leg to prompt a response and she gave her head a little shake as tears clouded her sparkling eyes.

"X, I don't know what to say. Selfishly I want to tell you not to go. I'm so scared of what will happen to you and I'll miss you so freaking much. What am I supposed to do when you're gone? I realize how immature that is and know you are going off to fight for our country. You'll be the bravest, strongest, and most impressive soldier. The Army doesn't understand how lucky they are yet but they will. I'm so proud of you!" She cuddled closer into my side and I wondered if she was trying to hide her tears. I knew this girl too well. Even if I wasn't clued in, her sniffles would have given it away.

I wrapped my arms around her and held on tight. "Wills, nothing bad will happen to me. I know how to protect myself and I'll have thoughts of you keeping me safe. This is just something I have to do, you know? To protect and serve. It gives me the chance to prove I'm more than just some kid. I'm not destined for college right away so this works out perfectly. Promise me you won't overthink this."

Her body shuddered with silent sobs so I lifted her chin to gain the attention of her emerald irises.

"Wills, I'm your best friend. Remember? I always know what's going on in here." I tap her temple for emphasis. "I will come back to you. Your friendship means everything to me but I have to do this. I promise to return in one piece so everything can go back to normal. Can you get on board with that?"

Willow bit her bottom lip before nodding slightly. More tears spilled down her cheeks before she collapsed into my embrace. I barely heard her speak so I couldn't quite make out the words but they sounded a lot like, "I love you."

My hopeful heart began beating erratically at the thought. Those words were on the tip of my tongue so it has to be my wild imagination playing tricks on me. Willow couldn't possibly feel the same way about me.

I may not have exactly kept my promise but we made it back to each other regardless. As I kiss the top of her head and snuggle her closer into my side, I realize fate must have planned it like this. We were always destined to be together but we had to redefine us first.

———◆———

LIFE IS STARTING to make sense again and I couldn't believe it. I have my Wills back.

I bet most couldn't be satisfied with a life out in the boon-docks but over the last week we kept plenty busy. We spent our time cooking meals, taking hikes, and playing Monopoly. I watched her knit several hats and I even agreed to model a few.

Willow read me excerpts from her smutty books and I tried teaching her the proper way to split wood. There was also plenty of fucking. Willow referred to it as making love, and damn do I love her, but I refused to call it that in my head. I was fucking crazy about this girl but wasn't completely ready to turn in my man card. I had to keep some of my masculinity or Willow would think I'd gone completely soft.

I quickly learned I'd do anything to see Willow smile and hear her laugh. Now, I'm so fucking gone that every piece of me belongs to her. I need to be constantly touching her because she soothes any jagged edge that threatens to surface. Waking up well rested with Willow wrapped in my arms took some getting used to, but now I need her sleeping next to me.

I would happily spend my existence just being grateful for having her in my space.

Our space.

With each additional day, the love in my chest burns brighter. The adoration and devotion I'd always kept hidden is finally broadcasted in high-definition. My heart is sparking with vibrant life now that my soul has bound to it's other half.

Shit, I am so fucking screwed.

At least that's metaphorically *and* literally. That immature thought has me chuckling to myself, which pulls me up short. Just a few short weeks ago, I was in a state of constant torment and now I'm laughing. Willow is a fucking miracle worker.

I'm so wrapped up in our exclusive paradise that I miss the signs Willow is practically waving in my face. She brings up her job frequently. She talks about the friends she met at school. Her apartment in the city. I'm blinded by the belief Willow is happy here and wants to stay with me.

Of course that isn't a fucking realistic possibility.

We're spending a lazy morning in bed, my fingers are stroking through Willow's glossy brown locks while she rests her head on my chest. My other hand is busy copping a feel of her tight ass. I'm peacefully drowsy while playing ridiculously cheesy scenarios out in my mind when Willow breaks the silence and my world crashes down in fucking shambles.

"I've been here for almost two weeks, which is all the time I could get off work. I've been meaning to bring it up but it never seemed like the right time. I can't avoid it any longer since I have to be back in the office on Monday." She sounds robotic while smashing my heart into pieces.

My body freezes in place and my palm stalls while sliding along her scalp. My muscles lock up and I'm sure my grip on Willow's hip is close to painful. My anger is fucking instant as reality seeps in. Just like that, she needs to fucking go. Guess there is no point in sugar-coating it.

The fury races up my throat as a roar escapes. "No! Fuck that bullshit. You can't go back. You need to stay here because I can't survive without you. It almost killed me last time." I don't care what I sound like. I need to change Willow's mind.

"Knock this shit off, Wills. You're happy here. I know you are. *I love you.* What more could you want? I've given you everything I fucking have!" I clutch her impossibly tighter and yank her head back so she can stare into my eyes while she destroys me.

Willow's overly expressive eyes flood with tears. "I love you *so much*, Xander. You know I do. I put my whole life in the city on hold. I can only take so much vacation time at once. I need to get back to my job. Those kids need me too. I can be back Friday night and stay through Sunday. That could be our regular routine until you're ready for more." She's crying while she talks, which causes her response to stumble out in a pile of garbled words. The outcome is the same regardless so it doesn't really matter. I already fucking lost her and she's leaving no matter what I say.

I start spewing shit right back at her. "That's all I've been to you? A fucking *vacation* from your real life? That's really great,

Willow. I'm glad I could fucking accommodate you. I wouldn't want to burden you further so you should leave now. Don't bother coming back either." I push her off me so I can sit up.

Willow's expressive eyes echo the excruciating pain currently ripping me. More tears flow down her cheeks as her throat works overtime to swallow her bullshit. I turn my back on her grief-stricken face as I edge to my side of the bed. I grasp my skull in my hands and squeeze in an attempt to alleviate the unbearable pain.

"You don't mean that, Xander. Don't do this to us. You said you love me." She places a gentle hand on my trembling shoulder. I thrash away from her caress as I stumble to my feet.

I whirl around and glare at her through narrowed slits. "I fucking love you so much that I breathe for you. You consume my every thought. You're alive *inside me*. We belong together so you need to stay here. It's not like I can fucking live in the real world. I need more time and I won't be all right if you're gone. Don't throw us away."

Willow is almost hysterical with hiccupping cries as I toss out that last ditch effort.

"I'll be back on the weekends. I'm not giving you an ultimatum like you're giving me. I stay here or that's it? There is no in between? People depend on me, Xander." Her words are a garbled mess but I'm hardly paying attention.

I'm not really hearing what she's saying. I'm blinded by the fact that she refuses to stay with me. Willow isn't comprehending my reasoning so why the fuck should I care about hers.

I suddenly feel rotten, fucking expired and all used up like moldy trash.

"Just fucking go, Willow." My statement is laced with venom. I am an imposter, a fucking fraud. I appear angry and furious when really I'm crumbling inside. My chest is cracking open as my fucking heart bleeds out. This woman is my entire world but right now she's gutting me. The edges of my vision begin to blur and my stomach clenches in fear that the demons are coming back for me. My neck is so tight that I start gasping for air. I need to get out of this suffocating house.

Willow is shaking her head as the tears flow nonstop down her blotchy cheeks. "Please, Xander. Stop and think about what you're saying. I just need to be gone for a little while, then I'll be back -"

"LEAVE!" I shout so loud my lungs burn from the effort. I cut off her blabbering because I can't hear anymore of her excuses. I was a fool to believe this all could be real. What a fucking cruel joke.

I spin away from her again and storm toward the door. I wrench it open before bounding down the broken stairs. Tears blur my own vision as I head for the sanctuary of the forest.

Fuck!

What the hell have I done?

thirty

willow

Once Xander stomps out of the cabin and apparently out of my life, *again*, I immediately jump into action. My heart begs my body to chase after him but my mind decides it would be best to leave this devastating situation. Even though I can hardly see what I'm doing, I stumble around the small house on autopilot while my eyes keep shedding tears. My insides are twisting painfully as I force myself to gather my stuff. My duffle is hastily packed and thrown over my shoulder in a few minutes before I'm striding out the door.

I hop into my car, which hasn't moved since I first arrived, and spit snowy gravel in my hurry to get gone. The road blurs in front of me since I'm crying so hard, which makes me feel reckless in a terrible way. The tires swerve off the road so I wrench hard the wheel, which sends my car skidding into the opposite lane. My foot slams on the gas and the rear end fishtails before I can correct it. I know how dangerous driving in my current condition is so I pull over on the next wide shoulder. The last thing I want to do is delay my departure but my responsible side wins out.

I give myself five solid minutes to let it all freaking out. I'm covered in snot and tears as I sob without limits. I bang my fists on the steering wheel as I curse Xander for being so inflexible. I scream at the injustice I feel and all the obstacles standing in our way. I'm consumed by overwhelming agony as I realize that this is probably the end for us. He was so freaking serious about wanting me gone. He wants to be nothing and my soul splits in half as the separation becomes reality. I am totally heartbroken.

How can I go back to the way things were before I reconnected with Xander? Like I don't know he's back and within driving distance. Pretend I don't know about his tattoo or the scars marring his beautiful body. As though everything we've exchanged didn't happen or was completely meaningless. Am I expected to just forget why he became a recluse? These depressing thoughts crush my pulverized heart even further.

I release a few more sniffles while I dig a wad of tissues from my purse. I dry my face and take some cleansing breaths so I can continue on my merry fracking way. My guts are drowning in misery while my body continues to fall down the bottomless pit of pain. My head aches from my nonstop sobbing and the exhaustion attacks my limbs. I am so ready for this day to be done.

After I've forced my mind to remain blank for at least thirty minutes, I'm able to get back on the road to go home. It only takes a few moments until thoughts of Xander slowly trickle back in. I reflect on how instant his hostility was triggered. As soon I brought up needing to leave, it seemed like a switch was flipped and the Xander I originally confronted was back in action.

There was no getting through to him and he shut me out before I could further explain my plan. I desperately wanted him to listen but his defenses were locked firmly in place. Xander didn't want to hear me because he was lost in the battle. I could almost see shutters slamming down over his ocean eyes and he became totally detached all over again. I wanted to yell and demand he stop the completely unnecessary regression.

I'm already filled with worry about how he will cope by himself. Xander believes no one clearly understands the magnitude of what he's dealing with, but he hasn't tried any therapeutic options lately. What will he do now?

My heart races as my mind conjures up horrible images of him suffering alone. He sounded so vulnerable that I wished so badly the rest of my days could be spent out there with him but that doesn't seem like an option anymore.

I understand that Xander's trauma plays an enormous role in his behavior but I figured we'd progressed beyond the point where it would be an issue. Why can't he trust in our bond? My chest burns and my stomach is a tangle of knots. I have no clue what to do. Completely removing myself from his life seems impossible so maybe I could offer support by utilizing my professional training. If he isn't interested in our romantic relationship anymore, perhaps he would be open to me helping him in other ways.

My chest constricts at the idea of going back to just friends, or even worse, but I don't see other options at this point.

———

Two days have gone by and time has only exacerbated the situation with Xander. Not like I've spoken to him but my mood continues to plummet the longer I'm away. Even though he carved a hollow cavern in my chest, my entire being aches for the man who effectively decimated me. I'm broken beyond freaking repair because of him but I can't help worrying about the jerk.

Every moment we shared plays on a continuous loop and I find myself constantly crying. I recall the lazy mornings when we resisted getting out of bed. The active afternoons full of long hikes and lost conversations we should have had years ago. I obsess over the endless nights of making love and finally being together the way we were always meant to. Those were the best days of my life and I fear I won't get more to cherish.

I've tried distracting my mind but my heart is banging a persistent beat that is hard to ignore. I miss him with such ferocity that I'm sure I'll never recover. I'm a total wreck as my life cracks further apart the longer I am away from him. I can't seem to do much of anything without wishing he was next to me. There is a Xander-sized hole in my life that no one else can fill.

I have a life here in the city, complete with a full time job and a mortgage on my house, so my responsible side pushed me to take care of my obligations. I quickly learned the error in my ways since I am useless without my heart. Life will always be where Xander is, no matter what crazy crap I tried feeding myself after I first left. I was upset and angry that he threw our love away but now I'm flooded with guilt. I've let him down and left him out there to struggle without anyone to support him. In my absence, he will allow the demons to regain their grasp.

I'm worthless at work, wasting precious oxygen. I'm here physically but mentally I'm back with Xander in the woods. I'm a zombie only awake courtesy of copious amounts of caffeine and the fact I can't freaking sleep.

My co-worker has me facilitating a group alongside her but I haven't spoken a word since I sat down. If I wasn't already feeling dejected, my counterproductive behavior would throw me off the ledge. I'm being a stellar role model for these teenagers.

I'm yanked out of my hazy musings when Lark claps her hands directly in front of my face. I jerk backward and almost topple out of the chair. My palm smacks over my mouth as I swallow a scream. My pulse is erratic and I decide this could be my tipping point.

"Seriously, Lark!" I whisper-yell so I don't freak out any of the kids. I glance around and realize we are the only ones in the room. "Wait. Where did everyone go?" The confusion in my tone is evident.

Lark huffs in annoyance before making a shooing gesture. "Let's talk in your office, Mopey. Get going."

I lead the way for our short walk down the hall. I open my door and let her through before taking a seat behind my desk. My hands are shaking so I clasp them tightly in my lap. When I glance up, Lark has an expectant look on her face.

"What?" I decide to go with an ignorance angle.

"Dude. What the actual fuck? I know you're a very empathetic person but sobbing in the middle of group is a tad excessive." Lark's potty mouth reminds me of Xander, which causes me to start crying all over again. When she notices my tears, she shakes her head and puffs out an aggressive exhale.

I wipe under my puffy eyes before responding. "I know, Lark. I'm a freaking disaster. Clearly. I just need a minute to get my crap together before I get back in the routine."

Her arched eyebrow and severe frown says it all.

"You need a lot more than that, honey. You've been wandering around here like you've lost your will to keep your head up. What gives? Don't you dare try to lie. I just watched you stare blankly at the wall for an entire hour." Lark's scowl becomes more pronounced the longer I hesitate.

I think it over and decide it might help to vent. She understands how important it is to process through difficult situations. Lark will tell me how it is and kick my butt into gear.

"So, remember when I told you about Xander?" I blurt the words out and cringe after uttering his name.

Lark releases a high-pitched screech that would send dogs howling for safety. "I freaking knew this was about a guy! Is that where you've been all this time? No wonder you're a hot mess. I want all the deets. *Spill.*"

Gosh, she is sassy.

Just talking to Lark brightens my mood slightly, whether I like it or not. I scrub my hands over my blotchy face before diving into my drama.

"Xander disappeared after heading overseas for his deployment, right? Well, I found out from my mom a few weeks ago that he was back in Minnesota. I had no idea since I haven't freaking heard from him after all this time. She convinced me to visit the house where he's staying."

Lark is happily eating up my words so I'm encouraged to continue.

"When I got there, it did not go well. Think of the Beast when Beauty first shows up. I was overjoyed to see him alive but he was an unrecognizable savage. He was horrible to me right away. All he did was growl and yell. We were best friends but the guy I used to know was nowhere in sight. After Xander got all angry and territorial of his privacy, I tried to leave. Remember when we got all that snow?"

She nods enthusiastically and motions with her hands to keep going.

"Right. Well, that was the day I spent over three hours getting there only to have him immediately turn me away. Worst part was, I ended up stuck in his freaking driveway. I'm talking wheel spinning, no way in heck I was leaving. Xander managed to pull his head far enough out of his butt to help me but it was a constant battle." I begin with that first hostile encounter and gradually unravel my past two weeks, making sure to gloss over the intimate details. I was willing to share but I wasn't one to kiss and tell.

Lark doesn't say a word the entire time I speak, except appropriately placed gasps and shocked exclamations. When I get to the final fight that caused me to flee, her eyes are glossy and brimming with understanding. Dredging up all those details leaves me more drained and exposed, which allows the hurt to rain down on me.

Lark puffs out a frustrated breath before crossing her arms in a defensive gesture. "This is exactly why I don't have a boyfriend. You get all dependent and . . . *blah!* Just look at how screwed up you are. You're so sad and glum but consider yourself lucky. People can't hide their crazy forever and Xander sounds like a tough nut."

"*Urgh*. That's real nice, Lark. Seriously, you know better than to make assumptions. Remind me why we're friends?" I scold her for picking on Xander but I know she's trying to be supportive. "And you don't have a man because you're a workaholic. Plus, you get bored easily and have no shame letting your insanity hang out. Don't tell me you've already forgotten about New Year's Eve." She's so ridiculous that I can't help letting a little laugh escape.

This girl might live for her job but that doesn't stop her from getting wild sometimes. I've witnessed Lark black-out drunk a few times, and let's just say she doesn't require privacy once she finds a guy that tickles her fancy. She also seems to attract drama in the form of girl-fights but whatever.

I'm thankful to her for lifting my spirits but once I take notice of my improved attitude, my stomach cramps and my chest tightens. I feel guilty because I'm sure Xander is struggling. My heart pleads with me to forget everything else and go to him. My mind scolds the pesky love-obsessed organ and reminds me that he made his choice. The worry still floats around me like a dense fog no matter what I think though.

Who does he have out there to help him?

Lark senses my downward spiral so she quickly intervenes. "You bring up a really great point. My job *has* taken over my life and I could use a break. And obviously you're in need of a serious distraction. We're going out for drinks. If we leave now, we can still catch happy hour."

"What? No! You can't be serious. Were you not listening to me just now? I'm not in the right frame of mind to be out in public. I couldn't even participate in group and I love leading those sessions. Plus, it's a freaking Tuesday." I refuse to spend the evening drowning my sorrows with booze.

"If we don't go, what will you do instead? Sit at home alone and think about Xander nonstop. How is that helpful? You need to escape for a few hours and loosen up. It will also give me a chance to leave the office before five o'clock for a change. Win-win! Come on, Willow." Her amber eyes plead with me and I can't find the strength to fight her. I really don't want to hang out in a bar but it does sound better than another night sobbing into my pillow.

"I have a feeling I'll regret this but all right. I'm mostly agreeing for your sake though." I tip up my lips in an attempt to smile but it feels super fake.

Lark is instantly giddy and eagerly bouncing in her chair. Her puppy-dog gaze is long forgotten.

She zips out the door before I can even consider changing my mind so I start packing up my stuff. My thoughts effortlessly drift to Xander and wonder what he's doing right now. I'm immediately swallowed by guilt when I imagine what he's going through, but he made it extremely clear he didn't want me around.

I'm not sure how long my responsible side will hold out against the gravitational pull to the boondocks.

I'm only so strong and I've always been weak where Xander is concerned.

thirty-one

xander

When I eventually dragged my stupid ass back to the house, there was a tiny part of me that believed I hadn't scared Willow off. Her missing car was a big fucking hint to her absence but I searched regardless.

Once I realized the place was empty, I went fucking nuclear and have been losing my shit ever since. Without Willow here, there is only darkness to keep me company. I immediately felt the abyss swallowing me up, without any intention of spitting me out.

The light is rapidly fading the longer she stays away. Everything looks fucking gray, which matches the dull pang ricocheting in my skull. My body is hollow and empty. I'm beginning to sink deeper into fucking nothingness.

I've officially lost my fucking mind. Everything is broken and dismantled. I've been altered irrevocably and am beyond the point of repair.

Physically.

Mentally.

Emotionally.

The booze doesn't stop the torment. Pushing my body to the point of utter exhaustion no longer works. The concept of time doesn't register anymore so who fucking knows how long I've been curled up on the floor. I can't fucking move other than to shake uncontrollably like I'm being electrocuted. The torture is extremely fitting.

The hallucinations race through my brain on a jagged cycle. Ripping through my unbalanced psyche and destroying any semblance of normalcy. The visions haunt me relentlessly and become more gruesome with every loop around. Hard to fucking imagine but these pictures are worse than before. Instead of my fellow soldiers, it's Willow dying. The woman I love being killed right before my eyes. Over and over and over again.

Brutal.

Inhumane.

Grotesque.

I can't fucking stand it.

I'm not strong enough to keep living when there is nothing to survive for. Willow kept me grounded but now I'm floating in toxic waste.

I'm at the end of my fucking rope and I'm losing the will to keep holding on.

The hate bubbles up my throat and I fucking choke from the acidic burning. It's no wonder she left. I'm a disgrace and don't deserve happiness. I allow the familiar destruction and loathing to wrap around me like a cloak, which effectively drags me deeper into the pit.

I can't go through this again so it's time to end this shit once and for all.

thirty-two

Willow

Going out was a terrible idea. All it did was loosen my already weak grip on reality. With a few drinks under my belt, my heart had the opportunity to take control of this freaking disaster my life has become. Soon enough, I was openly sobbing, in the middle of the bar, on Lark's shoulder. I tried my hardest to keep the crazy under wraps but once the flood started, there was no stopping the torrential downpour. Lark ushered me out and drove me home with strict instructions to head straight to bed. No more wallowing over Xander allowed.

Yeah freaking right.

I'm currently sprawled out on my couch, hysterical cries echo around the room as I mourn over the love I've tragically lost, while eating a pint of ice cream. Yes, I've turned into the typical cliché and proud of it. I'm not far enough gone that I don't realize how dramatic this behavior is but I simply don't care. I would gladly hop right back into Xander's arms if I wasn't scared of his rejection. His actions the other day practically destroyed me so I'm not super eager to receive another verbal lashing.

For now, I'll just pass the time blubbering like a scorned teenager. My biggest mistake was digging out the freaking scrapbook I'd made for Xander right after he left.

Why do I insist on torturing myself?

My finger traces along a picture that's bordered with pink sparkly hearts. I vividly remember selecting the edging with way too much thought. I graze some satin ribbon that edges the page and release a broken breath. All these details are ridiculously excessive.

With my beautiful craftsmanship on full display in front of me, the raw pain chews up my insides while my throat tightens to the point I can hardly breathe. He doesn't even know I made this collection of memories for him and I'd promised myself years ago it wouldn't resurface from the bottom of my closet. Alcohol had given me a different idea.

With streaks of tears pouring down my cheeks, I recall why I decided to make this enormous waste of time in the first place.

Xander had left a few hours ago and my heart was slowly breaking apart ever since. My stomach was a jumble of painful knots while my mind treated me to a nonstop replay of the stupid mistake I'd made. I should have told him I loved him and that for years I'd been wholly consumed with nothing but him. And now that Xander was gone, I was splintering apart from the inside out.

I couldn't survive without him.

He was always there for me during my emotional meltdowns but he wasn't here for this. My best friend was halfway across the world, preparing to fight in a war, and I couldn't find the freaking courage to tell him how I really felt.

I couldn't wait to talk to Xander. Maybe the thousand pound weight on my chest would ease up after I knew he was safe. His soothing voice would repair my fractured insides and calm the persistent worry slithering along my skin. I was ready to tell Xander I loved him, no matter what. I was done with the missed opportunities and debilitating regret. Even if he didn't feel the same way, relief would rush through me once I confessed my deepest desires.

Exhaustion pulsed through my body but my brain refused to relax. I needed something to keep me occupied while I waited to hear from Xander. Inspiration bolted through me like lightening and I instantly planned a gift for his first care package. After he knew how I actually felt about him, a scrapbook of all of my favorite memories will be the perfect sentiment to show him how deep my attachment flowed. An enormous smile took over my heated face when I imagined him opening the box and finding the token of how I truly felt.

It was absolutely perfect.

My momentary glee vanishes with the faded memory as the anguish once again dominates my weary soul. I'd never heard from Xander that day, or any freaking day for that matter, until I went knocking on his door years later. The brightly burning love I had for him slowly transformed into piercing disbelief the longer he remained silent. The scrapbook leaves a bitter taste in my mouth since it's a stark reminder that I've probably lost Xander all over again.

What happens now?

This destructive phase I'm drowning in can't continue and I'm ready for a solution. The only possible option for me involves Xander, and I refuse to make the same mistakes as I did before. I won't sit around and wait for him this time, which means I'll be heading back to the woods soon enough.

thirty-three

xander

Everything fucking hurts.

White-hot agony slices through my torso as my limbs shake with excruciating convulsions.

This must be hell.

Aside from the uncontrollable tremors wracking my arms and legs, I can't move. It seems fitting that I'm suspended in this paralyzing state of horrific torture. The end of my life should be an explosion of agonizing misery since that's all I deserve.

I choke on my next inhale, my lungs are burning like a blazing wildfire. Pitiful tears fall from my eyes and sear my cheeks like acid. I'm ready to face my eternal punishment for being such a coward.

The demons have won and they're coming for me. Just as my heart slows to a dangerously low beat, a bright flash flickers in my peripheral vision. Twisting my neck in the direction of the light sends a sharp pain down my spine but I've already gone mostly numb so I barely flinch.

My exhausted brain registers the sight in front of me before my eyes can gather enough strength to see through the inky hue coating my vision.

No.

No, no, no.

With what little strength remains in my weary body, I roll toward the blurry vision of Willow even though I hope she isn't really there.

Please don't let her be trapped down in this pit darkness with me.

My sweet angel doesn't deserve the brutal abuse I'll receive in the disgusting place I'm headed.

My teeth clench painfully as an agonizing slash rips through my chest when I attempt to move closer. My bleary eyes squint in a weak effort to focus on her fuzzy form. Black spots dance in my vision and my heart begins to race in sheer terror.

I can't fucking die now.

Not without protecting Willow from this hell first.

My muscles scream in fury as I force them to start working again. I can't handle the gruesome nightmare of her being locked in this dungeon with me. My last wish is to ensure her safety and it's that driving demand that forces my broken body off the floor. Willow needs me and I can't let go until I know she's free.

Blinding light engulfs the room as the haze in my mind clears. I stagger to my unstable feet with determination boiling in my gut. No matter what it fucking takes, I'll make sure the love of my life is sheltered from harm.

thirty-four
willow

Another dreadful forty-eight hours have passed where I've contemplated driving out to Xander's place over a bazillion times. I can't overcome the heavy weight of guilt from abandoning him out there all alone but it is so much more than that. Even with my mom's uplifting pep talks and Lark's continuous hovering, I can't be bothered to care about anything else.

There is a desperate urgency racing through my veins and I'm overcome with the need to have Xander's strong arms wrapped around me. I need to tell him how much I love him and how agonizing it's been since I've left. The fear of his rejection forces me to stay away. The uncertainty of Xander's feelings gnaws an enormous hole of doubt into my mind.

I worry about his reaction to my leaving and what he's doing now that I'm gone. If how he was living before I showed up is any indication, I have every right to be nervous. Xander was a complete wreck and I hate imagining him slinking back into that existence.

These daunting thoughts have been pestering me since I fled his house, and I'm slowly driving myself crazy. I can't sleep, I barely eat, and functioning at work is obviously not a priority.

Why did I feel the desperate need to return to the city? Why didn't I just stay with Xander? I should have known I couldn't withstand any separation between us.

During my stay in the woods, I knew Xander was ruining me, but at the time it was an amazing thing. I cherished the faithful leap my heart took and appreciated the trust reflecting back at me in Xander's eyes. I was irrecoverably his in every possible way. Now, that loyalty leaves me broken and useless. I can't function without him.

I've just resigned myself to driving to Xander first thing in the morning, when a startling pounding begins at my front door. My head whips to the clock on my nightstand to see it's 3:00 in the effing morning. Who is their right mind would be here at this time?

The nonstop banging gives me a sense of urgency so I jump into action without second thought. I peek through the side window but I can't see a darn thing since it's pitch black outside. I fumble for the light switch, but the glow isn't much help. The looming figure on my stoop in covered in shadows.

I unlock the bolts before gripping the knob to let my visitor inside. Once the door is creaked open, I get a solid look at the version of Xander I was terrified would return. His head remains lowered but I can see his entire form shaking and trembling uncontrollably. Despite everything between us, I've lost any hesitation when it comes to this man so I don't think twice before reaching out to him at the same time he steps forward.

I'm crushed against his quaking frame with my next breath.

As his arms band around me, the tension begins to slowly seep out and Xander sags into our embrace. His hooded head nuzzles along my hair as he clutches me impossibly tighter.

The agonized groan that vibrates from his throat causes my body to shudder. The noise that escapes him gives voice to his suffering.

"Fuck, Wills. You have no idea how fucking good this feels." Xander's voice is beyond raspy, as though he hasn't spoken a word in days. I clench my eyes shut against the sudden onslaught of tears when I realize the truth likely behind that thought.

He rolls his damp forehead against mine, which causes our noses to rub together. Every innocent touch is amplified due to our unwelcome separation. Xander clutches the fabric of my shirt in his tight fists as he draws me desperately closer, until no space exists between us.

Being held by Xander distracts me from all the pain our recent distant has caused. He's here now and his hands grasping my hips feels so freaking great that my heart is pounding uncontrollably. His fingers dig deep into my skin and somehow drag me even closer. It appears Xander wants to fuse our bodies, which I eagerly reciprocate by clamping onto him with all my might.

As we stand here, clutching onto one another like our lives depend on it, my lungs expand in a relieved sigh since I've never been happier. It dawns on me that no matter what, from this point forward, I will be by his side. The smile splitting my face is ridiculously huge but I could care less as I snuggle into Xander's chest.

With a deep inhale, I catch a whiff of something foul and cringe. The guilt slams into me all over again before I catch myself.

"How are you here? How is this possible?" My mumble is tinged with desperate awe.

What does it mean that Xander is at my house? His responding moan is a blend of relief and pain but either way he's here with me.

He shifts slightly to lay his jaw along the top of my head. "That is a long story, which I fully intend on telling. Can we go inside first? I'm fucking freezing and I can feel the panic rising out here." He sounds so sad that it cracks my already battered heart even further.

I'm already pulling him past the threshold as I utter, "Of course." I stumble backward through the entrance hall toward the bathroom. Our slow shuffle ensures our bond doesn't break as we near the door.

"There's so much to discuss but would it be alright if we shower? We can wash this horrendous week away and start fresh?" My suggestion seems to please Xander because he's already lowering my pajama shorts as we step onto the tiles. A small laugh bubbles out of me at his obvious hurry. "Would you prefer to take a bath or just rinse off quick?" I nod my head in the direction of the humongous tub that takes up half the room.

My question seems to yank Xander out of his haze and he halts our progress. He roughly scrubs a hand over his face on the way to lowering his hood. When his face comes into clear view, it takes all my control to stifle my gasp.

Xander looks like he's on the verge of collapsing. His eyes are painfully bloodshot and his lids are extremely swollen. The dark circles below are so pronounced, they look like bruises. Sweeping my gaze over the rest of his handsome face only proves how impacted he was by my absence. Xander looks wrung out and totally exhausted, like he's running on fumes.

He catches me staring but doesn't shy away. He traces the bags under my eyes with a gentle fingertip before speaking. "Looks like we match, Wills." My pulverized heart instantly soars as he connects our misery. It shouldn't be sweet to have this in common, but it only proves how deep our connection runs.

I'm sure he can see the hearts and stars in my eyes, which has him leaning down to place a delicate kiss across my chapped lips. I easily melt into him and quickly forget about getting clean in favor of absorbing his affection. Xander breaks away far too soon and I try to follow him to remain locked together.

"You pretty much told me I reek so let's take a fast shower, all right? Then we can . . . figure it out." His pause leaves a lot open for interpretation and my imagination takes off with the wide range of possibilities.

I'm nodding in approval as we begin undressing each other. When Xander lifts the hem of my shirt over my breasts, his dog tags come into view. The loud hitch in his breath signals his awareness before his fingers brush over the metal while lightly grazing my sensitive skin. His heated gaze lingers on my chest but he raises those gorgeous baby blues to my face when I clear my throat.

"I'll always be yours, X. Even if there are days we are apart, you'll always be with me here." I wrap my hand around his holding the tags over my heart to prove my point. "When I said I'd never take them off, I meant it. No matter what, remember?" My words are whispered but spoken with solid conviction that vibrates from my throat.

He leans further into my space before uttering, "I love you so fucking much, Wills."

His lips descend upon mine for a brief but passionate kiss that expresses how intense our bond is through the electrical current passing between us.

Xander cranks on the water after tossing my tank top to the floor. Based on the state of Xander's clothes, I'm not sure they will ever be suitable to wear again so I gladly remove the stained material from his skin.

We're naked in record time and then clumsily fall under the hot stream. I start rubbing soap along every inch of Xander's body before he returns the favor. We race through the motions in order to get the job done, only stealing a few sexually suggestive touches along the way.

When we've deemed ourselves clean enough, Xander tenderly wraps a fluffy towel around my dripping form before hastily wiping himself dry. My teeth are chattering from the chill in the air as I gaze at this amazing man standing beside me. I still can't believe he's here.

I so better not be dreaming.

Without a word, Xander scoops me into his arms before beginning his search for my bedroom. I give a helpful gesture in the correct direction and his long strides quickly bring us to the edge of my mattress. Xander glides me down his slippery skin while lowering my feet to the floor. Sparks dance along my flesh from the sensation as a shudder rolls through me.

My palms flatten against his pecs and I get lost in his molten stare. "I'm so glad you're here, X. I still don't understand how but I am extremely grateful. I was really struggling and planned to drive to your house in the morning, just so you know. I'm fine with spending the rest of the night cradled in your arms but we're going to talk about what happened soon. I bite my lower lip to trap the words I actually want to say. I desperately want answers but more than that I need to feel Xander's body connect with mine. I crave the intimacy that making love provides but I won't push it.

Xander scoffs before shaking his head, sending droplets from his wet hair flying. "Don't talk crazy, Willow. All I fucking need right now is to be buried inside you. Get your ass in bed so we can make up properly. Then we'll talk." He emphasizes his point with a sharp slap to my towel-clad butt. I don't need to be told again.

I hop onto the silky covers and scooch until I'm in the middle. I ease up onto my knees and beckon Xander closer with a crook of my pointer finger. He leaps at me, lacking any sort of grace, but the power behind his aggressive move boosts my raging arousal. He tries to take charge of the show but I push against his shoulders when he attempts to lay me down.

Xander follows my lead without any fight, and reclines his long body out next to me. He stretches his bulging arms above his head, which causes his ridiculously sexy abs to flex. I let an embarrassing loud moan escape because . . .

Dang, he's so freaking hot.

He's already hard as a steel pipe, his erection pointing directly toward those slabs of muscle on his torso. The swollen tip is leaking that makes my stomach grumble like I'm suddenly starving. I gladly climb astride his broad hips and align our most sacred regions. I wrap my fingers around his glorious shaft and slowly sink down until he's sheathed within me completely. I'm so freaking soaked that it hardly takes any effort, and the instant pleasure is so intense, my spread thighs quiver as my entire being sighs in bliss. My pussy weeps in desire, which eases the sting of being stretched so wide, but I still have to sink down slowly to allow my core to accommodate Xander's size.

His grip returns to my hips in a punishing hold as he groans low and slams his eyelids shut. "Shit, Wills. We gotta go slow or this will be over in a snap. I've missed you too fucking much." He grits out through clenched teeth. I'm already on the edge with him and I definitely want to draw these delectable feelings out.

As I begin a tantalizing rhythm meant to ebb our impending orgasms, I lean down to place supple kisses against the scars marring his chest. I glide my palms against his damaged skin and let my love flow into him with every caress. Our bodies are deeply connected as our souls become tightly entwined.

Hitched breaths and startled gasps surround us as we become consumed by our passion. I'm lost in the seductive strokes and hypnotic thrusts when Xander takes control from below me. He sits up and envelops me in an unbreakable hold. I'm still straddling him and this position sends him unbelievably deeper. Our bodies slide together like perfectly matched puzzle pieces.

My mouth hangs open in a silent scream as Xander alternates between whispering words of love and sucking along by jaw.

We continue worshiping and cherishing our reunion as seconds blend into minutes that make it seem like hours have passed. We're drenched and covered in salty sweat but still keep pushing forward. My pulse is vibrating an irregular beat while Xander surges further into my core. The tingles start sparking and radiating throughout my tense form. My inner walls began spasming and clenching, effectively crushing Xander's enormous dick inside me.

All of a sudden I'm on the brink way too soon, but that's what Xander does to me. When I catch his blazing blues, I can tell he's teetering on the edge of euphoria as well. While holding his unwavering stare, full of so much devotion, I let the release whisk me away. Once my body erupts in shudders, Xander leaps off the cliff with me.

We are waves crashing against ocean rock during high tide. Our climaxes join forces and blast through us. I feel Xander burst as his cum floods my fluttering pussy. My peak plateaus but the intensity doesn't waver. We clutch onto one another as we ride the electric current jolting through our charged connection.

Eventually I sag into his chest, utterly depleted but extremely satisfied. My eyes drift close as the enormity of what just occurred blankets over me.

Between heaving breaths I hear Xander whisper, "I see you too, Wills."

thirty-five

xander

I'm running my fingers through Willow's damp hair as she snuggles deeper into my embrace. She collapsed into me, greedily gasping for air after we screwed each other senseless. We haven't moved much since we are still trying to recover, which results in a naked Willow wrapped around me.

I'm one lucky bastard.

My eyes want to slam closed in utter exhaustion but I can't get my brain to shut down and my mind wanders aimlessly. The girl currently cocooned around me is my entire world but I'm still nervous as fuck being in an unknown space. Sleep has eluded me since Willow left my house so I'm probably bordering on delusional at this point.

The darkness tried to snatch me up for good and I didn't have the strength to continue struggling. Just as the black waters began drowning me, Willow saved me once again. I could feel her light beaming down into my deprived eyes before I heard her soothing tone float through the chaos. Willow's whisper was louder than any of the roaring hallucinations. It was her soft voice calling out to me that dragged me from that dank pit I'd been wallowing in.

I forced myself to find a way to her because I wouldn't survive another day without Willow's warmth. It wasn't easy hitching a ride into the city, especially in the middle of the night, but someone was clearly watching out for me. As I limped along the narrow road toward town, a trucker took pity on me and gave my psycho ass a lift.

I could hardly keep the panic controlled as we bounced along the freeway. My demons had a tight grip on my sanity but Willow's pull was stronger. I refused to surrender to anything or anyone except my beautiful Wills. Her encouraging words were playing on a continuous reel as I blankly stared outside the passenger window. *"Come back to me, X. I love you, X. I see you, X."*

Countless hours later, I had her wrapped in my arms and I could finally breathe again. I didn't anticipate Willow's impatience but I definitely wasn't fucking complaining when she started taking off my clothes. When she slid down on my cock, it felt like a fucking housewarming that I didn't deserve but I selfishly accepted. Her tight pussy squeezing the hell out of my dick was fantastic but her sweet words were icing on the cake. All night long we went at it until our bodies and minds were fucking spent.

This is heaven on Earth.

I release a lungful of air and Willow to stirs against me. I figured she had fallen asleep until her hand begins rubbing along my ribs. She presses a light kiss to my pec before nuzzling into my neck. Willow's tone is smooth as satin when she asks, "Xander?"

"Yeah, baby?" My reply is muttered against her forehead.

"Are you alright being here in the city? Are you alright? I was so worried about you, X. I want to know everything. Tell me what you're thinking about." Her voice is scratchy from screaming through our sex marathon, which has my chest puffing out in pride. Then her words register and my ego deflates. Willow isn't busy thinking about my mad skills in the sack. She's worried about my wellbeing because I'm fucked up and need help.

I release a frustrated groan. "When I'm with you, I actually get some semblance of normal. At least what I would consider typical. All the crazy shit stays quiet because you consume every part of me, Wills. When you bring up how I might be feeling in certain situations, I start getting fucking anxious since I know the darkness can easily trap me again. Right now, with your sexy body mashed against mine, I feel like a king. What'll tomorrow bring? I have no fucking clue." Talking about my black episodes causes my heart rate to spike and my muscles tense against a potential onslaught of panic. My palms had been stroking along Willow's back when our conversation started but now, both hands are formed into a tight fists against the mattress.

"Should we go back to the cabin?"

"Will you stay there with me?" My reply is harsh, even to my own ears.

Willow's fingers continue their soothing touch along my torso but her response has my defenses quickly rising. "Well, I can for a little while but I'll have to come back for work. I can't leave my job without giving them decent notice. That hasn't changed, Xander."

"Then I'm not going back." I inject as much strength as possible into my words.

"What? Why?"

"I can't fucking be separated from you, Wills. I can't do it. I need to be with you more than just on weekends. Even picturing life away from you gets me upset and freaked the fuck out. These past four days were absolute torture. I don't even want to discuss it, but know I refuse to live through that shit again." My breaths are puffing out of me in short pants as I get worked up imagining going back to my cabin alone.

Fuck that shit.

Willow's wandering hand stills against my sternum where my heart is racing wildly. "I would love for you to stay with me. I just assumed this wasn't an option. Of course it would be wonderful to live with you here but I want you to be happy, X. I need to be with you, too. More than anything, I've realized that now. If you hadn't come out here, I was going to find a way to stay in the woods with you. You're my life and I can't manage without you near me."

Hearing a similar declaration from her lips causes my soul to fill with pure joy. My weak limbs sag into the bed knowing she won't leave me again. I brush a swift peck against her temple.

"Being with you is all I need in this twisted life of mine, Wills. You're helping me flatten the erratic curves by just being with me. I owe you everything for that." I wish there is more I could say to get my point across. Wills was my entire universe and I would cease to exist without her.

Her exhale is stuttered and accompanies a few sniffles.

"You're such a great man, Xander. I love you so freaking much." She pauses a moment while her eyes shutter closed before flutter open again. "I kept trying to force you into the slot you used to fill and that isn't fair. We're both different people now and I'm so thankful for that. Maybe we needed to drift apart in order to slam back together. You know?"

I had no idea what she meant. There is no way she actually enjoyed the messed up parts of me.

"I'm not the guy you used to know. I'll never be him again, Wills. It sucks and I hate it because I never want to disappoint you. I want this to work out between us so fucking badly. I know we could have a future together because you're all I see and that will never change.

"I feel so much better just having you around. It's like you're a balm to my crazed mind. I don't feel like my skin is burning when you touch me. I can sleep. I actually feel relaxed. With you next to me, holding my hand, I believe anything is possible." This woman drags the syrupy confessions out of me without even trying.

I'll never get tired of telling her how I feel and she's earned an endless supply of sweet sentiments. Willow deserves much more than what my words provide and I'm hoping to have the rest of our days to prove myself.

She straightens her arms in order to hover over me. Her green gaze is still watery but beyond the surface, her irises are smoldering. I see eternity in her eyes as I get lost in her stare. That look alone liquefies my insides and I surrender all I have to this girl. I'd gladly offer anything I had to keep that level of love reflecting back at me.

Then Willow smiles and my brain shuts the fuck down. All that registers is the brilliant stunner blinding me with her light.

"Xander, you don't get it at all. I've always loved you and yes, you're a drastically different man now but that doesn't freaking matter. I see you in front of me and I want every single piece, no matter how jagged. Every crack, hole, divot, and defect is a part of you that I wouldn't change. Who you are today is the guy I'm confessing all my feelings for. This version of you has recaptured my heart and gives it reason to beat rapidly. I'm crazy about everything related to you, even the parts you hate." Willow interrupts her speech to smack a loud kiss across my lips before continuing.

"All mixed together, you're the perfect package that has me completely head-over-heels. No matter what you say, I think I would be disappointed to lose any side you have to offer." Unwavering devotion drips from her words and I know this is forever.

I crush her tiny frame into my bulky build. Our flesh snapped together like a powerful magnetic force.

We will never be separate again. I will make it my fucking mission to ensure nothing ever pulls us apart.

thirty-six

willow

With the morning sun comes the first day of the rest of my life. This time when I wake up, everything feels solidified and solved. It boggles my brain that Xander found the strength to leave the comfort of his house to show up at my place in the crowded city, full of everything that fuels his panic. If he hadn't already told me how much I mean to him, there wouldn't be a single doubt in my mind after that.

The level of actual ease his reclusive isolation brought him is debatable but being in a busy town must be far worse for him. I'm extremely impressed and it somehow has my already bursting heart expanding further. I finally understand what all those fairytales are made of.

Xander is perched by the stove while I cook some eggs. He claimed this would be a team effort but all he's managed to accomplish is turning me on by stroking any exposed skin he can find.

I can't forget the succulent kisses along my neck and shoulder. Or the way his massive arms tenderly intertwined around my middle to drag me back into his solid body.

Some people believe hugs are overrated but there isn't anything better than being wrapped up in Xander's embrace. It turns me into a gooey pile of mush which is why he's getting away with not helping me make breakfast. He deserves to be spoiled, right?

I was already planning to take today off work and I'm extremely thankful we have time to create a plan. Xander will live here with me, of course, but what is he going to do besides lavish me with attention? I'm hoping he'll be open to suggestions.

Once our meal is prepared and the table is set, I decide to bring up possible ideas. It's never been my intention to push Xander past his limits but after last night, I think he's ready to take more steps toward recovery.

I reach across the table for his hand and give it a little squeeze. "Have I told you how relieved and happy I am that you're here?" I feel like a dork once the words slip out but oh well. I can't help beating around the bush a bit.

Xander shoots me an odd look before releasing a disbelieving chuckle. "Wills, really? Just spit out what you really have to say." His sexy rumble has my lady bits perking up in excitement.

Maybe I should postpone this little chat in favor of something more . . . *pleasurable.* That sounds like loads more fun. Look at his handsome face and his piercing blue eyes. That shadow of scruff seems to highlight Xander's ridiculously angular jaw. His perfect pout curls up on one side before he tilts his heads slightly.

"Wills?"

Crap, he totally caught me ogling him. Again.

I scrunch my nose and squint at him slightly. My mouth is pinched tight as I prepare my proposition. "Remember our unspoken rule? You have to let me finish before you're allowed to jump in. This is important to me." I flash him a megawatt smile to take the edge off but it falls flat at the sight of his frown.

He huffs out sigh. "Let's hear it."

I don't know why I'm so freaking nervous to talk about this. I'm pretty sure my palms are sweating and that's just gross.

"I have a friend who works at the VA Hospital downtown and she told me there is a clinic attached where they offer a lot of support groups. I've been thinking how beneficial it could be for you to join one. You can find fellow survivors and people living through similar situations." I took a pause to gauge his relatively indifferent reaction. When Xander doesn't pipe up right away, I'm encouraged to give him more details.

"The awesome thing about a group setting is everyone tends to be at different stages of therapy. Some have already won the battle against whatever haunts them while others are just beginning. What they all have in common is the desire to find a solution so they can heal. They're taking action and seeking out the vital help needed. The support in numbers is stronger and wider spread. If nothing else, you could listen to their stories and success. Then you can decide if that option makes sense for you." I end my spiel with a long exhale. The air gets caught in my lungs as I wait for Xander's response.

It seems like hours have passed before he mutters, "Would you go with me?"

My response is instant. "Absolutely, X. I'll be part of everything in your life."

"Our life, Wills. We should always refer to it as ours from now on." His softly spoken words have my romantic heart racing.

I can't stop the goofy grin from spreading my lips.

"That is so sweet, Xander. You always know exactly what to say." I take a moment to appreciate this amazing man.

How did I get so freaking lucky?

I swallow the emotion suddenly clogging my throat before asking, "You're really open to trying the group?"

"I'd do anything for you, Wills. I'll try for you but also for me. I understand that I need to care about myself too. I want all those missing pieces back so I can be complete for you. For our future together. So yes, I will try to get better *for us*." Xander makes sure to emphasize those final words.

"Really? I kind of assumed you'd fight me on this, at least a little." I can't deny the stunned flutter in my chest.

"Why do you sound surprised? You should know by now that I'm willing to do anything it takes for you to believe in me again. I want you to be truly proud of me and I need to be a man deserving of your love. Wills, you're my end game. That's all there is to it." The finality in his tone leaves no room for argument. As if I would go against any of the wonderful things he's said.

This discussion suddenly reminds me of a similar conversation we once had. I giggle at the silly memory, which earns me an inquisitive glance from Xander.

"Do you remember that day I wanted to go horseback riding and you refused?" I toss the random question at him and watch as recognition dawns.

He nods before delving into the past with me. "How could I ever forget? You brought it up every chance you got. Always throwing in my face how badly I disappointed you. What a crock, Wills. You know exactly why I didn't want to go but I never fuck-ing lived it down." He scoffs in mock frustration.

I'm laughing so hard I almost can't speak.

"Oh my gosh! You were so freaking serious when you told me all that bouncing in the saddle would damage your *family jewels*. That your mother would be crushed if you couldn't give her grandbabies someday. Always thinking of others." Tears are streaking down my cheeks and my stomach is cramping but I can't control my glee.

"It isn't that funny, Willow. What made you even think of that? It was so long ago."

"You just said you would do anything for me and that wasn't always the case. See? You weren't so perfect back then, X. I much prefer this version that would take me riding if I wanted to go." I dangle my point in front of him to discover his reaction. I don't have to wait long.

Xander lets his mouth hang open before slamming it shut. He clearly isn't sure how to respond, so I let him off the hook easily enough. "Don't stress out. I was mostly joking but I do enjoy horses so it'd be fun. Maybe you could just stay on the ground while I ride." Being playful with Xander lifts my spirits to incredible levels. We used to cackle together on the daily so this brings back another long lost chunk of our history.

He visibly relaxes and snatches my hand back into his much larger one. "You're a brat, Wills. That obviously hasn't changed. If you actually want to go though, I would take you. I don't think I have the power to deny you anything." I could take advantage of his confession but instead, a calm washes over me because I feel exactly the same way.

"I love you so much, X. Thank you for coming back to me. Not just once, but twice." My eyes begin watering for an entirely different reason.

Xander slides his fingers through mine until our palms touch. "Thank you for saving me, Wills. Not just once, but twice." His bright blues sear into my glowing greens.

The final piece of our complex maze locks into place as our souls merge into one.

Our forever starts now.

epilogue

xander

Three Months Later . . .

Why am I so freaking anxious? These bubbling emotions are reminiscent of days I never want to recall but I am nervous for entirely different reasons now. I concocted this elaborate plan ages ago, before I left for the war. Willow has always been the one for me and I finally feel like the man she deserves. I'm ready to show my worth.

Thankfully, her parents are game and have been extremely helpful by convincing Willow that we're needed at their house on a random Saturday afternoon. This is corny as fuck, but today's the anniversary of when we first met. Back when we were little kids and weren't plagued with worries or responsibilities. We didn't have a care in the world except who to play with at recess. It was always Willow for me.

I managed to keep her from getting suspicious all week but once we arrive at her childhood home, her pesky curiosity begins taking over. She kept digging into the reason we're invited but I didn't let any details slip. It doesn't help matters when her parents remain very tight lipped throughout our stay. I could see the cogs and gears working overtime in Willow's brain.

I do my best to distract her by reminding her of our plans to go out later. She was shocked to discover I'd arranged a night out that evening and it worked momentarily. I made sure to include Lark, no matter how obnoxious she is, since she's become really close friends with her. Willow doesn't know it yet, but I want her surrounded by love tonight.

Being in public still freaks me out but I rein that shit in. I've made a lot of progress since Willow brought me back to life. With her by my side, anything is possible. I'm a solid example of the power of love's persuasion but it's obviously due to more than that. The guys I've met at the clinic have impacted my success immensely. I'm looking forward to hanging out with them to hopefully celebrate some big news.

We are slowly strolling toward the park as I continue reflecting on our recent time together. Willow and I go back to the cabin sometimes to make new memories. I gave her freedom to decorate however she pleased and she definitely didn't disappoint. The house now feels like a home, a place we can go to relax and enjoy being away from the busy city. I really enjoy those quiet times but I'm happy around her regardless of where we are. Most of all, I hope she wants to spend the rest of her life with me. We are about to find out one way or another.

As we near the swings, I hold the seat so Willow can hop on. I grip the chains so she doesn't move as I lean into her for a quick kiss. She tries to deepen the display of affection but I have a speech to get through. I break the contact between our lips but remain close enough that our mouths brush when I whisper, "I love you, Wills." She shudders subtly and it isn't from the mild chill in the air. Before she has a chance to respond, I drop down to one knee.

Willow gasps loudly and tears immediately fill her vibrant eyes. The green pools shimmer with devotion and speak louder than any words. I delicately grip her left hand in mine as I retrieve the small velvet box from my front pocket.

I clear my throat in an attempt to dislodge the lump forming. I can tell my eyes are expressing how emotional this moment is for me too.

"My sweet Wills, you are the love of my life. My fated destiny. You are my soulmate. My light in the darkness. You're my queen. The one I want to grow old with. My brave savior. You're my beginning and end. My absolute everything." I release a shaky exhale as I lift the lid to reveal the sparkling emerald-cut diamond solitaire. Her breath hitches and she straightens her fingers nestled in my palm. She's my eager girl too; I forgot to include that one.

"Willow Shae, will you marry me?" A lone tear trickles down my cheek when I finally ask the question I've been holding onto for far too long.

Willow leaps into my arms, which almost knocks me over, before shrieking, "Yes!"

I stand with her wrapped around me and spin us in fast circles. The next thing I know, we're kissing passionately in the middle of a children's playground. I give into my desperate need for a few moments before sliding Willow down my body. I clutch her tiny hand and slide the diamond ring onto her third finger.

What a sight to fucking see.

Once the physical representation of our engagement is settled into place, I gently kiss along her knuckle before catching her radiant gaze.

I stare deeply into the green eyes of my entire future. "I can't wait for you to be my wife."

the end

acknowledgements

SO, WHAT DID you think of my debut novel? I really hope you loved reading Redefining Us because I really enjoyed writing it. That means you'll be hearing plenty more from me, very soon!

Through this process, I've discovered that it truly takes a village, and my village is mighty.

First and foremost, I better thank my amazing husband. The real-life Prince Charming. When I told him I was writing a book, he was nothing but supportive. For the past several months he's allowed me to binge on social media. He's been patient when I would ignore him for hours on end while I was stuck in "the zone". Most importantly, he's the greatest father our little boy could ask for. Thank you so much, Honey Bunches.

I told my friend, T. Setela, I wanted to write a romance and she immediately told me to do it. She encouraged me right from the start and because of her words, I kept going. I trust her explicitly and her shove gave me the confidence I needed. I owe it to her that I have a completed novel to share with you.

Words will never describe how much I owe Ace Gray. She busted her bum to edit my book and did a phenomenal job. Her novels are sensational and the day I randomly stumbled upon Twisted Fate on Facebook will go down as one of the best. Her heaving, engorged folds are no match for my impaling penetration. You're the greatest, Ladyface!

My sister-from-another-mister, Chelle, has been fantastic as I got lost into the world of becoming an author. It isn't very pleasant to sit next to a social media zombie while we are trying to have fun so I really appreciate your patience. I'm so lucky to have her as my forever friend and don't know what I would do without her. I love you, MMM!

Lauren Blakely and Kahlen Aymes, you're the reason I started loving romance novels again, so many years ago. Your words inspire me every day and I will always cherish your friendship.

Ella James, you're a beautiful soul and I want to hug you daily. You brighten my life and your guidance is priceless.

AM Hargrove had an answer to every question and always knew the right thing to say. Your pictures and stories of Walter make me giggle, which only adds to your already heaping charm!

Thank you SO much Victoria Ashley, Penelope Ward, SL Scott, Cora Brent, Adriana Locke, Tori Madison, S. Moose, J. Daniels, Beth Michele, and M. Robinson for being there for me through this terrifying journey and allowing me to badger you with never-ending questions. The advice you provided me with has allowed me to feel more confident and comfortable in my new author shoes. You're wonderful and extraordinary!

JL Davis, I couldn't have survived without you! It is so difficult to find genuine people through an online connection and I'm so fortunate to have you. When I started my author journey, you were there from the start, holding my hand. I heart you hard!

The author community is extremely supportive and I owe you all so much for continuing to encourage me. A huge shout-out to Author Friends With Benefits and Indies Ink!

A special note to my fellow besties: Jen, Bobbie, and Margie . . . I love you ladies!

I owe Natalie (and Jennifer) from Love Between the Sheets big time so let me know when you're ready to collect.

Amy from One Book Boyfriend at a Time is truly wonderful and I'm so grateful for her help.

To my fellow bloggers, I know how hard you work for very little pay off. You make the author world go round so THANK YOU! I greatly appreciate each and every single one of you. I couldn't have done this without the support you all provide each day.

To the readers, you are the reason authors keep publishing their books. You are the life force behind this industry. You are simply spectacular. My gratitude to all of you runs very deep and I can't thank you enough for giving my debut novel a chance. Keep loving books for us, alright?

A huge thank you to my beta and proof readers. Proof This by Jen, Ace Gray, T. Setela, S. Killian, J. Gustafson, & C. Menden.

My formatting was done by Type A and they were amazing to work with. I owe them a lot for making my book look so pretty!

One last thank you to everyone that read Redefining Us. I greatly appreciate it! Reviews are the fuel for a book's success so I hope you consider leaving one, especially if you loved Willow and Xander's story.

Thank you all so much!

about the author

HARLOE HAS BEEN in love with romance since she was a little girl reading fairytales. The dream is to find the perfect person that completes your life, right? Novels have a way of bringing fantasy to reality and she's always up for an unforgettable adventure.

Harloe is married to an amazing man and they have an adorable baby boy. They are what make life worth living for her. Harloe has a day job that she loves and is also passionate about horses, blogging, country living, and having fun.

Redefining Us is Harloe's debut novel but there will be plenty more to come.

Stalk Harloe on her blog or send her a message at *harloe. rae@gmail.com*

CPSIA information can be obtained
at www.ICGtesting.com
Printed in the USA
LVOW11s1512210618
581477LV00005B/6/P